I0542392

'Til Death

DEADLY DECEPTION

KRIS NORRIS

Deadly Deception
ISBN # 978-1-78184-638-4
©Copyright Kris Norris 2013
Cover Art by Oliver Bennett ©Copyright June 2013
Interior text design by Claire Siemaszkiewicz
Totally Bound Publishing

Published in 2013 by Totally Bound Publishing, Newland House, The Point, Weaver Road, Lincoln, LN6 3QN

Totally Bound Publishing is an imprint of Total-E-Ntwined Limited.

DEADLY
DECEPTION

Dedication

To my brother, Norm. Thanks for listening to all my endless chatter about serial killers without suggesting I check myself into the psychiatric ward.

Chapter One

"You know, Mallory, if you don't stop fussing with your shirt, I won't be the only person in this room who knows that just being here is making your skin crawl."

Special Agent Mallory Reeves gritted her teeth as she released the fabric, glaring at her partner over her shoulder. Agent Cole Stevens smiled back at her, giving her a wink. Damn the man. Sometimes he was simply too cocky for his own good.

She turned to face him, allowing her shoulders to rest against the wall behind her. "Are you honestly going to stand there and tell me you enjoy being here?" She waved her hand at the small crowd gathered in the stuffy room. "It's like a fucking morgue."

"It's an execution. It's supposed to feel like a morgue. It's also one of the quickest turnarounds in history. I still can't believe Davies refused to appeal, if for nothing more than to drag this out longer. He could have easily spent the next decade in prison."

"Davies is sick. Nothing about him surprises me." She huffed, glancing at the people sitting in the front row. "And justified or not, his death won't bring them the peace they're hoping for."

"Maybe not. But sometimes closure is enough."

She swung her gaze back to Cole. "Would it be enough for you?"

"If it'd been my daughter that bastard had raped and killed?" He shook his head, stuffing his hands in his pockets. "I would have found a way to pull the trigger myself. But it wasn't, and I didn't let it get personal with this creep." He tilted his head slightly, letting his focus drop towards her ribcage. "I think the real question is…will it be enough for you?"

Mallory shrugged, trying to ignore the way the scar below her right ribs ached suddenly. "He stabbed me, Cole. He didn't rape me, or kill anyone I loved."

Cole gave her another smug smile. "Right. You didn't lose anything over this case but a litre or two of blood."

She cursed under her breath as he turned towards the covered window centred on the far wall. He obviously knew better than to mention Sawyer's name, but there was no mistaking the insinuation, and no denying the sudden flutter in her heart at the thought of her estranged husband.

Husband. How bloody ironic.

A secret wedding followed by an equally secret separation. And she didn't even remember the first part. But to make matters worse, while they'd been lovers for months, they'd never truly consummated their marriage, not to mention the fact she hadn't said more than a few heated words to him since he'd jumped ship two years ago, taking his life and her heart with him. And all because of that one night…

That one miscalculation that had not only ended the case but had nearly cost Mallory her life.

She released a slow breath but couldn't stop from searching the crowd again—reassuring herself he wasn't there. Though she felt certain he'd received the same notice, she'd known from the start he wouldn't make an appearance. Not here. Not for this.

Cole tapped her shoulder, motioning towards the window again. A low hiss of static sounded over the PA system, followed by the tell-tale scrape of metal on metal as the curtains pulled apart, casting a bright glare into the room. Just her luck that Washington State had finally caved to judicial pressure and allowed full disclosure of the event instead of the usual précised version. She could have handled having the bastard already strapped to the gurney with the IVs hooked up.

A hushed whisper rippled through the crowd as a set of large silver doors opened and a lone prisoner was escorted into the cubicle, his white scrubs nearly florescent in the harsh light. He looked exactly as she remembered him—long black hair slicked back from his face, deep lines around his mouth and across his forehead and the coldest grey eyes she'd ever seen. Every time she'd caught his gaze it'd been like looking at death.

John Davies shuffled to a halt, a cruel smile twisting his lips as he surveyed the gathering of people seated behind the glass. His gaze found hers and his smile flourished, flashing a set of crooked teeth. He didn't hide his contempt, just stared at her, eyes narrowed, his hands clenched into fists in front of him. She held his stare, vowing he'd be the first to look away. The unspoken challenge lasted several seconds until one of the guards pushed him forward, making him stumble slightly. He glared at the man over his shoulder, pulling his lips into a snarl, but the guard merely shrugged, angling Davies towards the gurney.

A cold fist settled in her stomach as she watched him climb onto the crisp, white sheets, his sadistic smile still firmly in place. Emotions she couldn't quite understand roiled through her, and she fought the sudden urge to run. She'd promised Cole, and her boss, she'd make an appearance—show Davies he hadn't beaten her—but as the guards reached for the straps at his wrists, tightening the leather bands around the thin expanse of flesh, she wasn't sure she could stay.

Mallory held her ground, trying to keep her focus on the event unfolding inside the sterile room, but she could feel a dark weight pressing down on her. She forced in a few quick breaths, not meeting Cole's gaze when he glanced at her, worry creasing his face. He mumbled something she didn't hear, turning to face her just as her cell rang. The hard beat of the music echoed through the silent room, drawing several disapproving glares. She winced, muttering an apology to Cole as she pulled the phone free and headed for the double doors just off to her left.

"Reeves."

"Mallory. Fisher. Sorry to call. I know the timing sucks."

Mallory inhaled a much-needed breath as the door shut behind her, blocking out the last of her thoughts about Davies. Some of the tension eased from her shoulders as she leaned against the wall beside the closed door, thankful for the unexpected reprieve. "Actually, your timing is perfect. What's up?"

A heavy sigh sounded on the other end, followed by an eerie silence.

She pushed off the wall, trying to ignore the rash of goose bumps that prickled down her arm. "Fisher?"

"We've got a body — Harbor Street — and...you really need to see this."

Mallory frowned just as the door whooshed open, nearly knocking her over. She looked across her shoulder as Cole stopped and stared at her, his face clearly displaying his concern. He moved to her other side.

"You do realise we're four hours away, right? Can't someone else field it?"

"I'm more than aware of where you are, but, the body, it's... Shit. You gotta see this to believe it. You, not another agent. And bring Cole. You're gonna need him. I'll wait for you two." Fisher breathed heavily into the phone again. "And Mal...this can't wait. Hell, it might already be too late."

"Too late? Fisher?" The line went dead. Her frown intensified as she pulled the cell away and shoved it in her pocket. It wasn't Fisher's style to be so cryptic, which meant she wasn't going to like whatever was waiting for her.

Cole motioned to her. "Care to share, or were you unhappy with the company in there?"

Mallory huffed, ignoring his dig. "Fisher wants us down at Harbor Street...something about a body we need to see. He says it's urgent."

Cole resisted her nudge, glancing back at the closed door. "We came for a reason, Mallory. Fisher can wait until we're done here. These things usually don't take more than half an hour, unless something goes wrong. And despite what he thinks, the body isn't going anywhere." He gave her a slow sweep. "Unless there's another reason you don't want to go back in?"

She scoffed, taking a few steps away. "As far as I'm concerned, the bastard's already dead. I don't need to watch him squirm."

"No. But those families in there might. Hell, we didn't come all this way just to back out at the last moment." His footsteps sounded behind her a moment before his fingers closed around her wrist. "You promised."

She glanced at his hand then drew her gaze up to his. "And you promised you'd respect my decision." She sighed, looking over at the door. "You know how I feel about..." She waved at it. "This. About him."

Cole pulled his lips into a thin line, apparently not missing the way she trembled slightly beneath his touch. "You could just admit you can't stand to look at him. To remember what happened that night. No one expects you to forget."

"No. But they expect me to continue to do my job, which becomes strangely difficult where he's concerned. That... Watching that isn't my job. Catching his ass was. A new case, however..."

"So you're not going to admit it?"

She flashed him what she hoped was a stunning smile. "And ruin your badass image of me? Not a chance."

She pulled her arm free and took two more steps before his voice sounded behind her again, stopping her in her tracks.

"I couldn't help but notice Sawyer didn't rearrange his life to be here, either. Are you sure this doesn't have anything to do with that?"

She cringed inwardly at the tone of Cole's voice. He wasn't holding back this time.

She glanced at him. "We both knew he wasn't coming."

"Maybe. But I think you hoped he was...for support. Surely he knew how hard this was going to be for you."

She laughed, shaking her head as she turned to face Cole. "Not as hard as facing me would have been for him. And even I know this isn't the place for that kind of *reunion*. But I figure since he can pull the invisible man routine, so can I." She motioned at the stairwell off to her right. "Now are you coming, or are you going back in there to watch a dead man die?"

Cole scoffed, nodding at her as they headed for the exit. "Fine. But if anyone asks, I'm blaming Fisher."

Lightning flickered in the sky as Mallory pulled into the narrow alleyway, parking her black Jeep beside one of the cruisers. Red and blue lights reflected off the rain, bathing the street with a strobe-like glow. Yellow tape blocked the way, enclosing the area in a familiar box she'd seen far too many times. They'd driven straight, the long trip unusually quiet. Cole had muttered a few token words, but it was obvious he wasn't pleased with her decision to ditch the execution.

She sighed. Just thinking about the creep made her shiver, though she'd never admit that to Cole, or anyone else for that matter. Davies was a weakness she needed to put behind her, and the sooner, the better.

Cole grumbled something under his breath about the weather ruining his leather jacket and the slew of cop cars blocking the road as he opened the door and stepped out, turning his collar up against the chill. Mallory followed, glancing up at the dark sky. April was usually one of her favourite months, but tonight, it had a desolate quality to it that made her feel lonely.

She sighed and followed after Cole, ducking beneath the tape as she made her way over to Fisher. He stood amidst a group of cops, a black sheet at his feet. She gave the covered body a quick glance, knowing just by the size and shape it had to be a woman, or worse, a teenage kid. The police officers turned as she stopped behind them, their faces clearly questioning her presence. She raised her badge and pushed through to Fisher, ignoring the looks the other men gave her.

"What's so important? While I don't mind your timing, I'm definitely going to catch shit over leaving the execution early."

Fisher nodded, murmuring a quick, "Hey," to Cole when the man rounded the sheet and stopped on Fisher's other side.

He pointed at the body. "In this particular case, I think the body will speak for itself." He knelt down and pulled back the cover, revealing bare, pale limbs and patches of pooled blood. "I also think this is going to make 'catching shit' seem a little less important."

Mallory drew a deep breath as she stared at the body—a young woman, no more than twenty-two, with blonde hair and even features. She looked more athletic than most, with firm limbs and a lean torso. But it was the pose that held Mallory's attention. Legs bent to one side with her arms raised over her head, the victim looked like a cheerleader jumping in the air.

The image hit Mallory hard, and she couldn't stop from taking a step back. Her gaze skirted over the body, unerringly going to every detail without hesitation—the ligature marks around her neck, the imprint of rope on her wrists and ankles, the trail of blood down her inner thighs. The only new element was a four-inch wound on the woman's right side, just below her ribcage.

Mallory shook her head. "Dear God." She circled around to her left, looking for more evidence, certain the one answer screaming in her head couldn't be correct. "From the look of the body, she's only been dead eight or nine hours... This... It can't..."

She looked away, staving off the sudden rush of emotions. She was obviously missing something—something that pointed this murder in a completely logical direction. It simply couldn't be what it appeared.

A hand settled on her shoulder, drawing her back from her thoughts. She glanced up, looking into Cole's dark brown eyes. They held the same disbelief she suspected hers did.

She took a deep breath, knowing he was waiting for her to speak but aware there wasn't anything to say. "It can't... I mean... Shit!"

Fisher moved over to her. "I had a feeling you might feel that way." He turned towards the dead girl. "Confusing as hell, really."

Mallory gave herself a mental shake. "There's bound to be a rational explanation for this. Obviously, we're dealing with a copycat here."

Cole huffed behind her as he knelt beside the body. "This ain't a fucking copycat and you know it, Mal. Look at the way the sash is tied around her waist. It's identical to the other twelve victims...same knot, same way he tucked the ends back underneath the fabric. We never released that information to the press."

"Shit gets out, Cole. You know that as well as I do. Someone could have shared that bit of information without us being any the wiser. Besides, the other victims didn't have a knife wound below their ribs."

Cole's gaze clashed with hers, his expression sending icy chills down her spine.

He motioned towards her. "You mean the same kind of wound you have? In exactly the same place? No, they didn't. But that just confirms our hunch. The bastard added that to mess with you...end of story."

Malloy sighed, palming her hands on her hips. "Okay. Let's say for one minute this isn't a copycat. Care to tell me how in the hell John Davies murdered this woman when he was fucking killed just hours ago by lethal injection?" She threw up her hands as she stalked around the body, shaking her head. "What the hell, man? How did he pull it off? He's been on death row for the last eighteen months. Let me guess...wormhole?"

Cole pushed to his feet as she stopped in front of him. "Damn it, Mal. I'm as angry and shocked as you, but you can't look at this woman and tell me her death isn't the work of that fucking psychopath." He held up a hand when she scoffed at him. "I don't have a goddamn clue how he pulled it off, but I'm certain of one thing. Nothing good is going to come from this investigation."

Mallory stared at the dead woman, Cole's words echoing in her head. She could deny it as much as she wanted, but he was right. Somehow John Davies had claimed another victim.

* * * *

Mallory reached for a mug, pouring herself another cup of coffee. The office was just starting to come to life, with agents ambling in. The grey light of a late sunrise chased away the shadows, taking some of her tension with it. Though it was hardly rational, something about the sun made everything seem just a bit less horrific, as if the light held some kind of magic.

Whatever it was, she welcomed the brief reprieve that had haunted her every waking moment since Fisher had revealed the body the previous night.

Footsteps sounded behind her and she turned as Director Don Henderson walked through the staffroom doorway, his shoes squeaking slightly on the polished floor. She gave him a smile as she leaned against the counter, knowing he wasn't here to simply grab some coffee or breakfast.

"Mallory."

"Sir."

He chuckled at the formality. Though she knew he preferred to be on a first-name basis with his agents, this didn't feel like the kind of conversation where she'd feel comfortable calling him Don.

He nodded at the mug in her hands. "Late night, or early morning?"

"More of a late night that turned into an early morning." She added some sugar, stirring it as she watched him over her shoulder. "Cole and I came back to go over some old files after Fisher's surprise last night."

"You two are stubborn like that. I think it's one of the reasons you work so well together." He poured himself a cup. "Come to any conclusions?"

"Just one. John Davies was a sick bastard who enjoyed killing and raping young women."

"I think we'd already established that. And seeing as Davies is dead…"

She nodded, leaning against the counter again. "I know. None of it makes sense. Cole's convinced this isn't a copycat, but unless Davies somehow got out of his cell, there's no way on earth he killed that woman. We've been searching the old records, trying to see if we overlooked anything—like the possibility of an accomplice—but haven't been able to find any trace that would suggest we missed a previous connection." She kicked her toe against the floor. "We'll have a better idea once the lab gets back to us. They think they might have gotten some DNA from the body. We'll compare it along with better images of the marks left by the rope and close-ups of the sash. If this is Davies' work, that'll confirm it."

"And if it points towards Davies, then what?"

"Well, it's a bit late to question the man, unless you've got better connections than I thought."

Henderson smiled, but it quickly faded. "Something tells me you wouldn't have been the first one in line to question him, anyway."

Their gazes clashed. She'd known that he'd eventually bring up the execution last night. "Probably not."

"Which brings me to the reason I came in here. I got a call from Captain Trevor Watts on the way here. You remember Trevor, don't you? The cooperative Chief of Homicide who provided invaluable assistance during our investigation. He went on about how the only two agents who had bothered to witness Davies' execution ditched the proceedings just as they were strapping the man to the gurney. Care to explain?"

She held his gaze, wondering if he'd already talked to Cole or Fisher. "The simple explanation is that Fisher called and said it was urgent. Since there were other officers present, I thought my time was better spent dealing with live criminals."

"Davies wasn't dead yet. What if the Governor had called and stayed his execution?"

"I considered that. But since it had about as much chance of happening as say, Cole getting a date, I figured the odds were in my favour."

A hint of a smile touched Don's lips. "Cole seems to think you couldn't stand staying there. That being so close to Davies got to you."

She arched an eyebrow. "Did he say that?"

Henderson scoffed. "Hell no. That man wouldn't give you up if you'd pulled your gun and tried to shoot the bastard through the glass. Let's just say I deduced it from everything he *didn't* say."

Mallory looked down at the floor. Why did it always come back to that night? "I think it's fair to say Davies' presence made me feel *uneasy*."

"I was thinking more along the lines of traumatised, but I'll go with your description for now." He moved closer, checking the doorway before focusing on her face. "You know, Mallory, just because you put this in the books a while back, doesn't mean you aren't still dealing with it. If you need more time —"

"I'm fine, sir, as shown by the fact I passed the psych eval almost two years ago."

"No one thinks you're crazy, but...let's just say John Davies cost you more than just a few weeks on the job." He straightened, taking a swig of coffee. "Cole told me Sawyer neglected to show up."

Mallory clenched her jaw. This was definitely not going in a direction she wanted. "Sawyer's two thousand miles away. Maybe there was traffic."

Don shook his head, the murmur of a chuckle drifting across the short space between them. "Right. Either way, he should have come...for more than one reason." He took another sip, looking at the coffee as if he'd never tasted it before. "Damn. I don't know how you drink this stuff."

"Iron gut." She took a deep breath. "If you'd like me to call the precinct and explain about last night, I'll —"

"No need. I already explained the situation." He dumped the rest of his coffee down the small sink behind her and headed for the door. "But if I lose to Watts on the golf course next week, you *will* be bringing me real coffee for a week."

Henderson gave her a smile and left just as Cole walked into the room. He gave the director a nod, raising his eyebrow at her as he headed for the sink.

"Henderson giving you shit for skipping out on the execution?"

"More like asking me if he needed to send me to the psych ward for a few days." She levelled a stare at him. "Somehow he got the impression I was creeped out by Davies last night."

"Weren't you?"

"Yeah. But he doesn't need to know that."

Cole held up his hands. "Don't look at me. I didn't say shit about that."

"Henderson said as much. But apparently you're not quite the blank read you think you are." She sighed, watching a bubble float around the edge of her mug. "Forget it. Let's just deal with the case. Any news from the lab?"

"Other than confirming the woman's identity to be that of one Susan Bach, age twenty, nothing. Basically, they nicely told me to fuck off and leave them alone to do their job. Said they'll call us when they've got anything remotely useful."

"Fantastic. Well, looks like it's back to doing things the old-fashioned way."

"I smell a road trip."

Mallory shook her head. "I wouldn't call canvassing the neighbourhood a road trip, but…" She held up her keys. "I'll drive."

"You drove last night. It's my turn."

"Doesn't your truck still have that check engine light on?"

Cole snorted as he headed for his desk, snagging his coat off the back of his chair. "Since when are you one to shy away from a dangerous situation? Nice deflection, but I'm driving."

"Have it your way. But that means you're buying coffee."

"Just don't spill any on the leather seats, okay?"

Mallory swatted him on the shoulder as she walked by, knowing it was probably the last easy moment they'd have until Seattle's latest killer was caught.

Chapter Two

Mallory palmed her head, trying to rub away the growing headache. After hours of scouting the area and a few more talking with the victim's family, they hadn't been able to confidently add a single person to their list of possible assailants. And seeing as their prime suspect was sitting in the morgue, there was little to go on.

"It's four o'clock. Why don't you just call it a day and head home? I'll call you when forensics has any news."

Cole's voice ghosted over her and she looked up, smiling at the warm brown eyes that met her gaze. He was a large man, well over six feet, with bulging muscles and black hair. His mocha-coloured skin accentuated high cheekbones and perfect long lashes she'd wished for on more than one occasion. But it was always his eyes that intrigued her, deep brown and brimming with intelligence and compassion. He was, without a doubt, her best friend.

She leant back in her chair, accepting the handful of pills he gave her. She reached for her water bottle, downing them in one gulp. "You've been here the same amount of time and I don't see you grabbing your keys."

He shrugged. "Yeah, but we both know I'm tougher than you so..." He chuckled as he dodged the wadded-up paper she threw at his head.

"Jackass."

"Ah, but you say it so nicely."

She pushed to her feet, ready to launch her water bottle at him when Director Henderson walked over to her desk.

She gave Cole a sideways look then turned towards Don. "Something on your mind?"

"I need a few minutes of your time." He waved in the direction of his office.

Cole tapped him on the shoulder. "Just her, or do I get to come along, too?"

Don shook his head. "Mallory's right. You're a jackass."

"But I'm your star jackass...sir."

Mallory rolled her eyes. "Just one question, Don. Should I bring a notepad or a lawyer?"

He grimaced. "Just come on in."

She looked over at Cole, but the man simply shrugged and followed the director into the room. She sighed and pushed her chair back, hoping her legs didn't wobble as she moved down the aisle, slipping past the door Don held open for her. She headed for his desk, taking a spot beside Cole as the man shouldered against the far wall, gazing out the window towards the park across the street.

Don angled the door on a forty-five then walked over to his desk. He didn't ask them to sit, just eased into his chair, grabbing a mug as he leant back. "Quite a mess we've got on our hands with this new…development."

Mallory scanned the room then settled on his face. "Quite honestly, sir, it's a bit early to panic. All we know for sure is that a woman's dead and it has similarities to another string of crimes."

Don chuckled. "Similarities? Damn, Mallory, are you sure you don't want to go into politics or something? 'Cause you sure do talk the talk."

"It's not just talk. Though I know my partner has doubts, it just doesn't seem possible that John Davies was in any way connected to this murder. And I stand behind our original findings." She moved closer, palming her hands on his desk. "That son of a bitch was as evil as they get. Not only did he rape and kill those girls, he enjoyed doing it. Every piece of evidence we found linked him to those murders, not to mention the fact we caught him bent over the last victim's body!" She pushed away, resisting the urge to draw her fingers down her scar. "The bastard confessed for Christ's sake, not to mention refusing every attempt at an appeal. So regardless of this *recent development*, his sentence was justified, no matter how you look at it."

Don sighed and shifted forward in his chair. "Easy, Mallory. I didn't bring the two of you in here to question your competence. In fact, it's quite the opposite." He cleared his throat, taking a swig of coffee before meeting her stare. "As you can imagine, Washington has quite a vested interest in how we proceed with this investigation. With Davies' body still warm in the morgue, they're hoping that we'll do everything in our power to keep the details of this case, shall we say, private. As such, they've decided to appoint a small, three-man team to head this undertaking—"

"So just like that, we're off the case?" Cole stepped forward, his massive body taking up most of the space on Mallory's side of the desk. "What kind of bullshit is that? High profile or not, nobody knows Davies' MO like us. Hell, it'll take a new team weeks just to go through his old file—"

"Cole. If I may finish."

Cole grumbled something under his breath but nodded, finally taking a seat in one of the chairs.

Don ran a hand through his hair, giving Mallory an exasperated look. "As I was saying. Headquarters in DC has picked a team, and they'd like the two of you to be part of it. As you mentioned, Cole, no one knows Davies like the agents who worked the original case. I have a feeling that knowledge will be indispensable in this matter. So effective immediately, you're to forego any other cases and ensure all your resources go to putting whoever did this in jail." Don looked them both in the eye. "Any questions?"

"Just one." Mallory leant forward, resting one hip on the edge of his desk. "Why did you bring us in here to tell us? Seems you could have just mentioned it in passing at our desks?"

The man fidgeted at his desk, shuffling papers as he mumbled beneath his breath. He finally raised his gaze to her, an apologetic smile gracing his lips. "As happy as you are to be part of the team, there's a small aspect that might cause some friction."

Mallory furrowed her brow, not sure where the director was heading, when Cole cursed and slapped one hand on his leg. She turned to him, eyebrow raised in question.

He gave her a knowing look. "The third guy."

She glanced from Don back to Cole. "Third guy? What are you talking about?"

Cole motioned towards Don. "Don said Headquarters was putting together a three-man team. And if they want agents who worked on the original case, then..."

"Ah, shit." She glared at Don. "They requisitioned Carter, didn't they? Damn, he's a whiny, arrogant jerk. I personally celebrated the day he transferred." She sank into the other chair and ran a shaky hand through her hair. She'd hoped she'd never have to work with the man again, but...

"Mallory."

She looked up as Don's voice broke through her thoughts. She met his gaze, not sure if he was amused or agitated. "Yes, sir."

"Carter isn't part of the team. He quit and went private a year ago, shortly after leaving here. And you're right, the man's an ass."

Mallory sighed then felt her breath hitch in her chest. There'd only been a few agents involved with the Davies case, and if they hadn't picked Carter... She forced herself to swallow as she stared at the director. "So who's going to be the source of my...displeasure?"

"That would be me."

She froze, the familiar deep voice starting a chain reaction in her body. The quick breath she'd been taking stalled, lodging tight in her chest as the hairs along her arms prickled to life, following a cascade of goose bumps across her skin. A rolling motion rumbled through her stomach, fluttering back and forth as a warm feeling took root in her groin. Her nipples hardened against the confines of her bra as a searing heat crept up her neck and into her cheeks.

And despite everything she'd told herself for the past two years, a sense of relief washed over her.

She heard Cole curse again as his chair scraped back and he rose to his feet, nudging her in the shoulder. But she couldn't move—still couldn't breathe—and she knew if she tried to stand now, she'd make a fool of herself and fall flat on her face.

A heavy sigh covered the short distance, sending an unwanted pang of desire pulsing through her. Damn, the man could still make her tremble with nothing more than a word or a sound. There was just something about his voice, dark and gravelly, that short-circuited her brain and put all her resources into preparing her body for a loving that would never come.

Old feelings resurfaced, and she pushed to her feet, clenching her jaw as she turned, instantly pinned by his blue eyes and sexy half-smile. She ignored the sudden pounding of her heart, praying he couldn't see the way her pulse thrashed beneath her skin. Two years, and he hadn't changed, other than looking better than ever. His hair was slightly longer, teasing his eyes as he pushed a hand through it, tousling it about his head. His shoulders blocked out most of the door behind him, making the room seem smaller than when she'd first entered, and his jeans still hugged his lower body like they'd been painted on his skin.

Don moved out from behind his desk, walking over to doorway. He extended his hand. "It's been a while, Sawyer. Good to see you."

Sawyer glanced at her again, his gaze travelling the length of her body, before darting back to the director as he shook the man's hand. "I'm not sure *good* is the word I would have picked, but thanks, it's nice to see some familiar faces."

Don turned towards her, his mouth pulled tight. "I realise this situation may be a bit *uncomfortable* at first but...there's not much any of us can do about it. The orders came directly from Washington, and they weren't in the mood to discuss any changes." He looked at Sawyer. "If I were you, I'd tread very lightly. The lady's been practicing a bunch of that mixed martial arts bullshit, and quite frankly, she's damn good at it. That, coupled with a memory befitting an elephant...not a good combination where you may be concerned." He slapped Sawyer on the shoulder, glancing back at her. "Mallory—play nice. And if you have to shoot him, make sure you use Cole's weapon. You're much easier on the eyes than he is." Don chuckled at Cole's muttered rebuke and stepped through the doorway, pausing halfway. "Just for argument's sake, there isn't anything I should know about the two of you that didn't come to light after the stabbing, is there?"

Mallory flicked her gaze to Sawyer before focusing on Don's face. "Like what?"

Don shrugged. "I don't know. Maybe something along the lines of you two getting married?"

Her stomach fell to her feet as she fought to keep her expression even. She forced in a gentle breath as she tilted her head slightly to the side. "Married? We haven't seen each other for the better part of two years. Don't you think that if we'd done something as foolish as that, one of us would have ended it by now?"

Don scrutinised her face, swinging his gaze over to Sawyer before swearing under his breath. "Fuck. You know what? Forget I asked. 'Cause if this blows up the way I think it might, I want plausible deniability."

With that he left, leaving a sudden void in the room. Mallory shifted restlessly on her feet, not sure if she should stay or push past Sawyer and head back to her desk, praying a hole would open up and swallow her.

Sawyer cleared his throat, at least having the decency to look slightly uncertain. He glanced at Cole, then back at her. "So. You really into that mixed martial arts stuff now?"

She raised the corner of her mouth into a grin. "Eighteen months. Just had to wait for my ribs to heal enough."

"Weren't you badass enough before?"

Sadness tumbled through her stomach, but she tamped it down. "It's like that old saying. You never know what you're going to need until one day you turn around and don't have it." She tried to shrug off the uneasy memory of that night as it clawed at the edges of her consciousness. "Now I have it."

Sawyer's mouth drew tight at her words. He sighed, leaning against the door as he continued to stare at her, his gaze repeatedly running the length of her body. She didn't flinch, wondering who would look away first, when Cole snorted and walked to the door.

He stopped beside Sawyer, patting the man on the shoulder as he turned towards both of them. "As much as I love being in the middle of awkward situations...I think I'll head back to my desk and let you two fight it out on your own." He gave her a smile before looking at Sawyer. "I'll be right outside if you need anything."

Sawyer watched Cole leave, glancing at her when he'd disappeared beyond the glass panels. "He'll be right outside? Jesus, Mal, what the hell does he think I'm going to do?"

She chuckled, resting her ass against Don's desk. "Actually, that comment was for your benefit, in case you thought you needed him."

Sawyer arched his eyebrow. "Me? Then I suppose the question is, what does he think you're going to do to me?" He nodded at her. "Attack me with some of your new moves?"

She waved her hand in the air to dismiss the notion. "Don't be silly. I wouldn't attack you, Sawyer." She narrowed her gaze on him. "I'd just shoot you."

He flashed her a wide smile, accentuating the dimples in his cheeks. "Now, darling. That sounds a bit simple for your tastes."

The endearment sent another shiver skittering down her spine, and she had to squeeze her thighs together to keep the empty feeling growing in her groin from taking control. Despite what her body clearly wanted, there wasn't a chance in hell she'd do more than glare at him, not when she already knew the outcome.

She sighed, resting more of her weight against the desk. "I've grown to appreciate the simple things in life. Less chance of them turning around and biting you in the ass."

The vein in Sawyer's temple danced as he took a few steps forward, closing the distance between them. "Technically speaking, I believe it was you who wanted the marriage annulled. I just got out of the way."

"Two thousand miles out of the way. And I believe I simply asked you to reconsider the arrangement until my damn memory returned. That entire day is nothing more than a blur at best."

"Oh, so I was supposed to just pretend that the most important event in my life never happened? That we never said any vows? Nice, darling."

Mallory huffed, spearing her hands through her hair as she fought the urge to pull it out—or strangle the man standing a few feet away. How he always managed to turn her words around mystified her. "That's not what I meant, and you know it. Damn it, Sawyer, between the trauma, the blood loss and the damn drugs, all I remember from that day are snapshots of lying on the pavement, your hand covered in blood as you tried to hold my fucking side together. I know we'd talked about marriage before, but... I don't even remember going to the chapel, let along signing those papers a few days earlier. I mean, damn, you have to wait like—what—three days or something?"

The lines around Sawyer's mouth tightened.

Mallory frowned. "Sawyer?"

Sawyer cursed, slamming his hand against the doorframe. "I wanted it to be a surprise. No friends. No family. Just us, together, at city hall. That's what you said you wanted if you ever got married. We were going to have a huge party after. So sue me for using my connections to *acquire* the permit so we could be spontaneous. It's not like I could have drugged you and forced you to marry me. But, for the record—that morning, you said it was 'incredibly romantic'. Your words, darling."

His words hit Mallory hard, stealing what little breath she had. God, if he only knew how wrong he was... Or maybe how right. She crossed her arms, not willing to back down. "I don't doubt that it happened that way, that I was fully coherent and willing. It's just... Shit. All I remember is waking up in the hospital ten days later, married, but with nothing more than a note saying you'd left. How the hell was I supposed to feel?"

"Convenient how you forgot the part where you freaked out on my ass and demanded the judge *undo* it."

"I was hooked up to morphine. I can assure you I didn't have any idea what I was saying or why I was saying it."

"You seemed to remember everything just fine after the surgery. You even told me how pretty the ring was. Then it was as if a few days later you came to your senses or something. You went ballistic, acting as if I'd somehow tricked you. And I think you made your feelings perfectly clear, morphine or not, so I gave you the space you obviously wanted."

"I didn't want space. I wanted—" She clamped her mouth shut, refusing to bring up what was better left unsaid. She took a deep breath, allowing some of her anger to dissipate. "You know what? Let's just forget it. Ancient history, as they say. We'll just pretend like we actually enjoy being in the same room together, and as soon as we catch this copycat son of a bitch, you can run back to Albuquerque and work on your tan."

Mallory took a step, planning on walking past him, when Sawyer moved with her, blocking her way. Any pretence of a calm façade had vanished, leaving his face creased with raw emotion.

"You're not going anywhere until we settle this."

She stood her ground, more than ready to knock him on his ass, when Cole appeared in the doorway.

"Hate to break up the reunion, kids, but forensics just called. They're faxing over their preliminary findings." Cole motioned towards his desk. "Now are you two actually going to do some work, or should I call the paramedics, just in case?"

"No need. I think we're about done here. Isn't that right, Sawyer?"

Mallory glared at Sawyer, nodding to Cole as she followed his lead.

Sawyer grabbed her arm as she darted past him, stopping her within an inch of his body. He crowded her against the doorframe, his warm breath tickling the shell of her ear. "You can run, darling, but don't get any wild ideas that this is anything close to being done."

She turned her head, ignoring the way his lips caressed her jaw as he slowly pulled back, keeping his mouth within kissing distance of hers. A surge of desire seared through her veins, followed closely by overwhelming hurt.

"You've got it all wrong, baby. You're the one who runs." She pulled free from his grasp, taking a much-needed step away. "Now if it's all right with you, I'd like to get back to work."

Sawyer let her go, mumbling something under his breath as she walked to Cole's desk, pulling a chair over as he waited beside the fax machine. She could feel Sawyer staring at her, but she ignored it, keeping her gaze centred on the spot between Cole's shoulder blades. A volley of emotions roiled around inside her, and she didn't know whether she wanted to beat Sawyer senseless, or beg him to fuck her against the wall. It'd been two years, but he was still the one—the only one.

Cole grabbed the papers and sank into his chair, shifting his gaze between her and a spot just beyond her left shoulder. He furrowed his brow, silently asking if she was okay. She gave him a smile, nodding at the sheets in his hands.

He shook them. "Okay, let's see what they found." He placed them on his desk, his fingers tracing the notes. "Time of death between six and seven p.m. No useable prints. Rope was standard nylon available from any hardware store. No particulates found in the knife wound—they're still determining the composition of the matter found under her nails and in her hair, but there were minute traces of latex, possibly from gloves." He sighed as he skipped down the page. "Wait. Here it is. Two distinct DNA samples were found. One was too damaged to get results and proved inconclusive. The other is a confirmed match—" His breath hitched and held as his gaze raised to hers. He grimaced and pushed to his feet, taking a step away before turning and handing her the sheet. "To John Davies."

Mallory stared at the sheet, the name typed in black mocking her. Her knees buckled and she plopped into Cole's chair, her fingers still fisted around the paper. "Impossible. It's just fucking impossible."

Cole sighed and moved over to her. "Now, Mal—"

"Don't patronise me, Cole. For God's sake, we were standing right there in the room when they brought the bastard in. Are you honestly trying to tell me that six hours before he was out killing this girl when the rest of the world believed he was eating his last meal of greasy take-out?" She ran a shaky hand through her hair. "He is dead, right? I mean, they called it...after the injection?"

Sawyer stepped closer to Cole's desk, entering her peripheral vision. "Don't you know? You just said you were there."

Shame hunched her shoulders as she shifted her gaze slightly. "Fisher called just as it began, and I couldn't bring myself to stay and..."

She didn't finish, cringing at the pleading quality to her voice. No wonder the director knew how she felt. She had a neon sign tattooed across her forehead.

Cole cupped her shoulder. "He's got to be dead. Short of the second coming of Jesus, no one can survive an overdose of sodium thiopental. But just in case, that's why the doctor's present. To declare time of death. Besides, the first thing I did after we saw the body in the alley was have the morgue confirm his identity. He's there, black body bag, tagged toe and all." His gaze shifted towards Sawyer before looking back at her. "You know I think you're the toughest badass in this joint. Hell, most of the time, I figure you're the one protecting our asses. But if you're not up to this…I get it, Mal. Like I said last night. No one expects you to forget."

She gave him a smile, ignoring the concern flashing in Sawyer's eyes. "I'm fine, I just… It's like trying to put a puzzle together only to realise you don't have any of the edge pieces. None of this makes sense." She stood, handing Cole the report. "And with a mug like yours, there's no doubt you're the brawn in this relationship." She dodged his attempted slap on the shoulder.

Sawyer moved closer. "Let's just think about this for a moment. There're really only a few possibilities. First, John Davies has an evil twin running around carrying on his work."

Mallory snorted. "I think that would have come out during the first investigation, but, yeah. I guess it's possible. What else?"

Sawyer shrugged. "John Davies has us all fooled and someone got him out of jail, rigged his death to appear real, got a lookalike body for the morgue and is now harbouring his creepy ass, or we've got a copycat on our hands who has samples of Davies' blood, DNA, you name it. Maybe a technician or reporter or, I don't know, janitor from the original case—someone who had access to him while he was in jail."

Cole nodded. "Right. So our perp—" He held up the paper, pointing to the bottom. "This inconclusive sample...gets some of Davies' blood, hair and skin and plants it at the scene, doing a perfect imitation of Davies' method, including details not released to the press—which is a mystery all its own, but whatever. The real question is, for what gain? Now that Davies is dead, the murderer has to know Davies will be eliminated from our list of possible suspects, even if the killer leaves a pool of the creep's blood at the scene."

"Maybe it was some kind of protest against his death?" She shrugged and leaned against the desk. "Or a tribute to his demented work."

Sawyer stepped forward, stopping dangerously close to her. "Or maybe we're overlooking another possibility."

She met his gaze. "What possibility?"

"That our original assumption on Davies' case was wrong."

"Which assumption? The batshit crazy part or the stone cold killer part?"

"The part where he worked alone."

Mallory shook her head. "Cole and I went through the old records, looking for that. There wasn't any evidence that pointed along those lines, and it's not usually the case in serial killings. Only a small fraction of these kinds of killers work with an accomplice. And Davies was obsessively meticulous about every aspect of his presentation. Having a partner would have made it extremely difficult to stay true to that design at the level Davies displayed."

"Maybe so, but it fits. That's how our guy knows what pose to put the girl in, how to tie that stupid sash...how to mess with us by leaving Davies' blood at the scene." He leaned against the desk beside her, brushing his thigh against hers. "It's just a theory, but the last time I checked, ghosts didn't bleed."

Mallory expelled a long, slow breath. The sleepless night was definitely catching up with her. She glanced from Sawyer over to Cole and back again. "Okay, looks like we've got a few theories to test. I'll go over the records from the jail. Maybe there're some leads on someone he served time with or visitors that may have wanted to stage an act like this. Cole, you cross-reference suspects from the old cases against any connections we have to Davies since his incarceration." She paused, finally looking up at Sawyer. "I guess that leaves you to go over the previous files and see if Cole and I missed anything last night that might point towards an accomplice. It was pretty late, so..."

Cole grabbed his chair, dragging it across the floor in front of his computer. "I'm on it."

Sawyer tapped her thigh, sending a rush of heat surging through her. She stared at where his fingers curled around her pants, suddenly wishing there was nothing but skin and sweat between them. The image burned her cheeks and she didn't quite meet his gaze as she turned to him.

"Problem?"

Sawyer rubbed her thigh again. "Just that I don't have anywhere to work."

She finally dragged her focus up to his face, immediately wanting to smack the sexy smile off it. "I suppose you can share my desk. Grab a chair and sit on the other side. All the files are in that folder. I just hope you find something we missed, because right now, our prime suspect is a spectre."

"Does that make us those meddling kids?"

"Only if I can be Daphne. Velma's got that bad haircut and she's always losing her damn glasses."

His gaze swept down her body, pausing in all the right places before slowly travelling back up. "Oh, you're Daphne, all right. And I know exactly why Fred wanted in her pants."

Mallory shook her head, picked up the folder and slapped it against his chest. "Just get to work. And if you're lucky, I'll try to remember why I shouldn't throw random objects at your head."

Chapter Three

Sawyer Kent scrubbed a hand down his face, fighting off the yawn that had been threatening for over twenty minutes, as he dropped the folder on the desk. He'd been staring at the files for hours, but hadn't been able to find the lead he'd been hoping for. If Davies had been working with an accomplice, the man had done a brilliant job at hiding that fact.

Sawyer leant back in his chair, looking over at Mallory. She'd lasted until about ten minutes ago before she'd palmed her head in her hands and closed her eyes. Though he was certain she'd only intended on taking a short break, her obvious fatigue had taken precedence, and she'd fallen asleep with her head nestled in the crook of her elbow on top of her desk. Even now, he could just discern the soft steady sound of her breath as it fluttered the stray wisps of chestnut-coloured hair about her face.

He clenched his jaw. This wasn't how he'd ever envisioned a reunion. Hell, he wasn't sure he ever had. After the breakdown she'd had in the hospital room, he'd vowed never to hurt her again. Yet here he was, two feet away, watching her work herself to the point of exhaustion, mostly because she didn't know how to handle his presence.

That and because she was as stubborn as a mule.

A hand curled around his shoulder and he turned, looking into Cole's penetrating gaze.

The man nodded at Mallory. "I told her to go home hours ago but…" His voice faded as he stared at the floor, toeing the tiles with the tip of his boot. "Guess I should wake her up and take her home."

Cole shifted his weight when Sawyer snagged his arm. Cole lowered his gaze, staring Sawyer square in the eyes.

Sawyer gave him an apologetic smile. "Sorry. I just wanted to say that you don't have to worry about Mallory. I'll see she gets home safe."

Cole's eyes narrowed as he looked from him to Mallory and back again. An amused grin curled one side of Cole's mouth as he took a step back and crossed his arms on his massive chest. "You're going to see her home?"

"And that seems strange because…"

"Because until five hours ago, your name was a curse word in this office. Christ, Sawyer, the two of you have barely spoken to each other since the case ended, but everything else went for shit two years ago. I thought for sure she was going to hurl that paperweight on Don's desk at your head." Cole chuckled as he shook his head. "I just hope you're up for the battle."

"There isn't going to be a battle."

"Isn't there? So I'm the only one here that feels the oppressive tension between you two?" Cole uncrossed his arms and stuck his hands in his pockets. "Let's be honest. Either you two are going to kill each other, or you're going to have the hottest angry-sex known to man."

Sawyer sighed. He'd forgotten how direct Cole was, though that was one of the traits he liked most about the man. And probably one of the reasons Cole and Mallory got along so well. Cole didn't take any of her shit, and Mallory had the heart of a saint, finding forgiveness in just about any circumstance.

Don't count on it.

Sawyer cursed at the nagging voice in his head, turning his attention back to Cole. "Is that why you think I'm offering to take her home? So I can have angry-sex with her?"

Cole shrugged. "Angry, hard, kinky...I don't think the type really matters." He held up his hand to stop any protest. "Hey, it's me. I watched you two fall in love and I know, at least for Mallory, those feelings haven't gone away. Just do her a favour. Think about more than one night before you jump back into bed. She hasn't done so well since the last time you were here. I'm not sure she can take another desertion. And don't get all defensive about how she wanted the marriage annulled. I'm just stating facts, not placing blame."

Sawyer glanced around the office, thankful they were the only three agents still left on the floor. "You know about that?"

"Are you kidding? I'm her partner. We spend an exorbitant amount of time together. I know everything." He chuckled. "Women like to talk."

"So this isn't you trying to put the fear of God into me if I touch her?"

Cole smiled and grabbed his leather coat off the back of his chair. "I'm not quite a god, but if that's how you see me..." He gave Sawyer a pat on the shoulder as he moved past him. "Just see she actually gets some sleep. A person can only go so long on whisky shots and long naps."

Sawyer watched the man amble down the aisle before glancing back at Mallory. He didn't like the picture Cole had painted of her life, but he supposed he wasn't the right person to criticise her. Not after walking out like he had. It'd been impulsive, hurtful...childish. But at that moment, he hadn't been able to handle her apparent rejection and had taken the easiest exit route—a transfer to his old unit in Albuquerque. Looking back, he was pretty certain he'd overreacted. Hell, he'd just plain fucked up.

He pushed to his feet, unsure of his next move as he gently shook her arm. She mumbled something cryptic and settled in again, more hair falling across her shoulders. It was longer than he remembered but just as soft as he trailed his fingers through the ends, wanting nothing more than to bunch it between his hands as he claimed her mouth.

The image made him take a step back. Cole was right. The last thing she needed was a quick romp with him. Hell, from the looks she'd been giving him, it was more likely she'd cut off his dick than allow it anywhere close to her body. And he couldn't really blame her. He'd been an ass. He still was.

"Mallory. Come on, darling, I'll take you home."

Mallory jumped when his hand settled on her shoulder again, blinking a few times as she gazed around the office. She squinted for a moment then groaned, running a hand through her hair as she leant back in her chair.

She looked up at him. "How long was I out?"

He smiled, wishing he'd taken more time to watch her while she'd slept. Appreciate the way her long lashes brushed against her pale skin or how her lips twitched when she mumbled something in her sleep. "About ten minutes."

She glanced over at Cole's desk. "Where's Cole?"

"He called it a day, which is what I suggest you do." He stood, grabbing her keys off her desk. "Come on. I'll drive you home."

Mallory stared at him, one corner of her mouth lifting into an amused smile. "I'm a big girl. I can drive myself home."

"Not without falling asleep at the wheel." He waved off her scowl. "Please. Whether you want to acknowledge it or not, I know you. You get this dazed look on your face when you're trying to keep your eyes open. And right now, I'm surprised you haven't fallen face first back onto your desk."

Mallory released a slow breath, shaking her head. "I haven't slept for two days. Yeah, I'm tired, but—"

"No buts. Regardless of your opinion of me, I'm not about to let you saunter off and get yourself killed because you were too proud to accept my help." He held up the keys and shook them. "Besides, I've got your keys."

"Jesus, you act as if I'm drunk."

"Driving in your state would actually be worse than if you'd been drinking." He motioned towards the door. "Grab your stuff and let's go, before we're both too tired to drive."

Mallory got to her feet, grabbing her coat from the floor where it'd fallen off the back of her chair. "But what about your car? Even you can't drive two at a time."

Sawyer clenched his jaw. He wasn't exactly sure where he was headed with this. He only knew he wasn't prepared to let her go just yet. "They roused me out of bed at four o'clock this morning and had me hop, skip and jump my way north just to get here. I didn't have much time to prepare."

"In other words, you don't have a car."

"No car."

She nodded, walking over to him. "So what's the plan? Take me home then head off to the hotel? Were you going to pick me up again in the morning?"

He tried not to flinch as he shifted his feet. "Like I said…not much time to prepare."

Mallory snorted as she rested her ass against a desk. "You don't have a place to stay yet, either."

"I was kind of hoping you might consider letting me stay in the guest room. Just for tonight," he added when he thought her eyes might bulge out of her head. "I'll find a motel tomorrow."

Mallory looked away, the muscle in her jaw flexing as she clenched her teeth together. "I sleep with my gun." She turned back to him, crossing her arms on her chest. "Are you sure you think being in the same house with me is a good idea?"

Sawyer moved closer, brushing his chest against her arms. "Are you planning on shooting me tonight?"

She smiled sweetly at him. "The thought had crossed my mind."

"There'd be a mountain of paperwork involved, darling, not to mention the bastardly job of cleaning up all that blood."

"Right. Wouldn't want that." She sighed, nodding towards the door. "Fine. You can camp out in the spare bed for the night. But considered yourself duly warned."

"I'll wear my Kevlar vest, just in case."

She chuckled and headed for the stairs, nearly tripping down the seven flights to the ground floor.

Then she made her way outside, walking across the road to a small parking lot. The attendant nodded at her as she darted through the gate and over to her Jeep. She rounded the hood and stood waiting on the passenger side as Sawyer unlocked the SUV and jumped behind the wheel. She slid into the seat and buckled her seatbelt, closing her eyes before he'd even backed up the vehicle.

Though it'd been a while, Sawyer made his way towards the house they'd once shared, the familiar feel of the road stirring emotions he'd hidden away. It seemed as if every tree and street corner brought back a long-suppressed memory, making him realise how empty he'd felt in Albuquerque. He had had friends, but...

He glanced at Mallory. Her head rested against the window, and her eyes were closed, but he knew she wasn't sleeping. Her breathing hadn't deepened and every now and then her eyelids fluttered open, revealing a hint of blue in the flashing streetlights. She didn't seem overly tense, though he suspected she wasn't quite prepared for him to spend the night, even if it was forty feet away with a couple of walls and a gun between them.

A thought flickered through his mind and his heart raced in response. He tried to take a calming breath as he cleared his throat, drawing her attention. He smiled, wondering how to ask the question without coming across as a jealous stalker. "So, you mentioned you sleep with your gun. Don't suppose there's anything else I should know? Something or someone else who might try to kill me if I get up to grab a glass of water in the night?"

Mallory's skin crinkled slightly around her eyes as her mouth curled into a knowing smile. "Is that your subtle way of asking me if I have a lover?"

He glanced over at her. "It wasn't subtle."

"Then the answer won't be either. There's nothing to worry about. I'm the only one who might take a shot at you."

He arched a brow. "Are you sure about that?"

She scoffed at him. "Am I sure if I have a lover? Yeah, I'm pretty sure I don't have one." She looked out the window at the passing scenery. "Cole stays the odd night in the spare room, but that's it."

"Is there something I should know about you and Cole?"

Her head spun around and she looked at him as if he'd lost his mind. "Are you seriously asking me if Cole and I are lovers?"

"You spend a lot of time with him, so it's only natural..."

"Natural that we what? Screw each other?"

He shrugged. "It happens, Mal."

She huffed. "Yeah, I know. No, we aren't lovers. I already tried sleeping with my partner once." She paused to look him in the eyes. "You know how well that turned out."

He tamped down the guilt that surfaced, nodding in silence. Yeah, he knew first-hand how that had turned out...not at all the way he'd hoped. He swallowed, turning onto her street. "So, no lovers."

"None."

"Currently or..." He motioned with his hand, unable to get the words to form on his tongue.

She laughed and shook her head. "None. Period. Ever. Are we done?"

"Can't blame a guy for asking."

"No, but I don't see you offering up any information."

"You didn't ask."

She glared at him. "That's because I have what they call tact."

Sawyer pulled into her driveway and cut the engine, spinning in this seat to face her. She might not have asked, but he hadn't missed the stressed tone in her voice. She was just as curious to know if he'd had any lovers as he'd been about her.

He looked her in the eyes. "I haven't so much as been on a date."

"You don't have to go out on a date to fuck someone."

He smiled at the provocative look in her eyes. "No, you don't. And I haven't done either." He nodded at the house. "So can we go in now, or do you need a blood sample for testing?"

"Can I use my gun to get it?"

He just stared at her.

She shrugged, giving him a hint of a smile. "Fine. Maybe later."

She opened the door and jumped out, stumbling again as she headed for the porch. He could see her fatigue hunched in her shoulders and wondered how she managed to stay upright. She fiddled with the key a few times, then slid open the door, casting a wedge of light across the tiled entry. He followed her in, squinting as she flicked on the light, illuminating the room in a harsh glow.

He looked around, placing his bag beside a small table. "Either you have a very fastidious maid or you don't spend much time here."

"I don't have a maid."

"That's what I thought." He pointed at the walls. "You painted."

"I had some time on my hands. You hungry?" She pointed at the kitchen. "There might be something edible in there, though I'd check the expiration date first."

Sawyer tsked as he toed off his shoes and moved over to her. "I thought you knew how to take better care of yourself."

"I'm fine." She leaned against the wall. "But I'm beat. Everything is pretty much where it used to be. There are towels in the hall closet if you want a shower. And you can repay me for my kindness by buying breakfast tomorrow. Now if you'll excuse me…"

She pushed off the wall and turned towards the hallway, stopping when he gently gripped her arm. Heat seared through his fingers and across his shoulder, spiralling down his spine and straight to his cock. God, how many times had he wished to hold her just one more time? To feel her skin against his as she pulsed around him, screaming his name like she'd done a thousand times before.

He pushed the thoughts aside, praying she didn't glance at his crotch. "Thanks."

"For what? You haven't made it through the night…yet."

"Maybe not, but…you could have tossed that paperweight at me in Don's office."

"It's heavier than shit. Besides, his son made it for him and he'd have my head if I broke it." She looked down at where his hand still held her arm. "Just get some sleep. It might be the only chance we get for a while."

He nodded, releasing her arm as she headed down the hall, drawn to the simple beauty of her. Even exhausted she was sexier than any woman he'd ever met, and he still couldn't believe he'd lost his one chance at claiming her as his.

Stupid damn case.

John Davies was the reason they'd got in this mess in the first place and it seemed the bastard wasn't finished with them yet. But as he listened to her door click shut, he vowed he wouldn't make the same mistake twice, if she didn't decide to shoot him in the night.

* * * *

Sawyer rolled in the bed, trying to get comfortable as he stared at the neon numbers mocking him. Two-thirty and he hadn't been able to get more than an hour's worth of sleep. He'd drifted off easily enough, but then he'd wakened shortly after, thoughts of Mallory haunting his every breath. Damn, what was it about her that drove him crazy? Made him want what he knew he couldn't have?

He cursed and stared up at the ceiling, wondering if she was having the same problem. He hadn't heard a sound from her room since she'd closed the door behind her a few hours ago, suggesting she'd given in to her fatigue and was peacefully sleeping away the night...like he should be doing. But every time he closed his eyes, her body materialised in the dark. Long and lean, with pale skin and taut muscles, every inch of her excited him. From the soft spot behind her knee to the rough patch of skin on her elbow. She was beauty in every sense of the word, inside and out, and he couldn't stop from picturing the two of them together again. Feeling her body give beneath his as he pounded into her from above, or holding her close as he took her against the wall. Any place, any way, just as long as he got to love her.

Love. Right. Like she still loved him. Hell, he'd spent the past two years wondering if she ever had. He just couldn't understand why she'd reacted so violently in the hospital if she'd had any kind of love for him. And morphine or not, she hadn't faked the hurt he'd seen in her eyes… Or had it been fear? Either way, he'd left, and now he didn't have a clue how to make his way back. He slammed his hand on the bed, wishing he could just say what he wanted to say to her, when her scream rattled the walls.

The sudden noise spooked him and he tossed the blankets aside, grabbing his gun off the side table as he rushed the door. He stopped, fisting the handle before cracking it open. He scanned the hallway then darted through, heading for her door. Her voice sounded again, words he couldn't quite make out, and he had to fight the urge to storm into her room, knowing if she was fighting an intruder, being careless could bloody well get her killed.

He halted at her door, pressing his ear against it. Mumbled words and squeaks drifted through. He took a deep breath and threw open the door, barging into the room with his gun tight in his hand. He cleared the area, checking the closet and bathroom before running over to her bed. She thrashed on the mattress, sweat beading her brow as her hands twisted in the sheets. Another ungodly scream vibrated through the room, and he reached forward, shaking her arm.

Her eyelids flew open, but she didn't stop fighting. She looked at him, glassy-eyed, fear making her pupils larger than usual.

"Mallory!"

She pulled against his hold, trying to roll across the bed. "No! Please."

"It's okay, darling. You're just dreaming. Wake up!"

She yanked her arm away, reaching for the opposite bedpost. He swore under his breath and jumped on the bed, pinning her in place as he held her shoulders, forcing her to look at him.

"I won't tell Mommy, just please, Daddy, don't!"

Her words sent a cold shiver down his spine and he shook her again, fear beading his flesh with goose bumps. "Damn it, Mallory. Wake up!"

His voice echoed in the room and for a moment she stopped fighting, staring at him in utter confusion. Then she blinked and swung her head from side to side, looking around the room as if seeing it for the first time. Her ragged pants filled the air and he couldn't do anything other than sit there, his legs straddling hers, his hands gripping her shoulders.

She sobbed twice then looked up at him, tears gathered behind her blue eyes. "Please. Sawyer. Get off me."

Though she'd barely whispered the request, it hit him full force. He stared at her for a second then nodded, shifting his weight so she could climb out from under him. She swung her legs over the edge of the bed, gripping the sheets until her knuckles turned white. She gave him a parting glance then stood up, rushing from the room without looking back.

Sawyer stared at the empty space below him, wondering what in the hell was going on, before shuffling off the bed and following her out. He stalked down the hallway, drawn to the sound of glass clanking in the living room. He stopped at the entrance, watching as she tipped a bottle of whisky into a small glass, her hands shaking so badly half of it spilled along the top of the bar. She didn't seem to notice as she lifted the glass to her lips and downed the liquid in one gulp. Then she poured another, repeating the process until she'd consumed three shots.

She paused on the fourth, closing her eyes as if just now feeling the effects of the drink. Sawyer leaned against the wall, one eyebrow raised in question as she turned, her gaze meeting his across the dark room.

She lowered the bottle, taking only a sip of the whisky before placing the glass on the bar. Her body trembled despite the way she tried to draw herself up, raising her chin in defiance. "Don't start with me, Sawyer. I'm not an alcoholic."

"Four shots in thirty seconds. Nope, no worries there."

She glared at him, finishing off the last of her shot as if proving her point. "It was called for."

He straightened, walking into the centre of the room. "Why? So you could numb yourself and not have to deal with what the hell just happened in there?"

"I am dealing with it."

Sawyer pointed at the bottle. "No, you're drowning it. There's a difference." He sighed, running a shaky hand through his hair. "You know, Cole mentioned something about you living on whisky shots and long naps. I thought he was joking, but apparently not." He took a step closer. "Care to tell me what that was all about?"

She met his gaze with a look of pure fury. "I had a nightmare."

"No shit."

She huffed, staring at the ceiling as if it held the answers. "I'm just wired with the new case and all this bullshit about Davies mocking us from beyond the grave. I'm fine."

"You're not fine, and this had nothing to do with Davies, unless you're into some kind of kink I'm unaware of."

"What are you talking about?"

"You just begged your father to stop...so unless you've suddenly started calling men *Daddy* this isn't about Davies or any other creep you've put behind bars." He gentled his tone, making his way over to the bar. "I think there's something you need to tell me."

Fear creased the fine lines around her eyes. She glanced away then dodged to her right as she tried to dart past him.

He caught her arm, careful not to hurt her as he pulled her back, forcing her to look at him. "Mallory. We were partners for years. Lovers for ten months. I need to know."

She shook her head, trying to pull herself free. "No. You don't. It's like you said. It has nothing to do with the case so...just let it go."

"And watch it eat you alive? No. Whatever it is, you won't heal from it until you embrace it. And you do that by telling me what the fuck your father did to you to make you scream out in terror."

She sobbed again, snagging her bottom lip as if hoping it would give her strength. He eased his hold, letting her lean against the edge of the couch as he copied her stance against the bar.

He ran a finger down her chin, wiping the tears that had trailed down her cheek. "Darling. Please. Talk to me. I know you grew up in foster care, so I'd assumed your parents were both dead, seeing as you never mentioned them. I'm starting to think that assumption was premature."

She huffed, finally raising her face to look at him. "Oh, no, my father's dead. Has been for twenty years."

"What about your mother?"

Shame bunched the muscles in her shoulders and she glanced away again, a heavy sigh marking the silence between them. "She's alive."

"Does she live in Seattle?"

She chuckled. "In a matter of speaking." She turned back to him. "She's in the Washington Correctional Center, serving a life sentence for murder."

Sawyer swallowed hard, suddenly unsure if he really wanted to hear the story. Something warned him that he was about to get more than he'd bargained for. "Shall I assume she killed your father?"

"That would be a correct assumption." Mallory sighed again, easing more weight onto the arm of the sofa. "You really don't want to hear this."

"But I think you really need to tell me."

She simply nodded, looking at the floor again. "My father was a drunken, abusive bastard who took great pleasure in making my mother's life a living hell. From the time they got married, he beat her...at least that's what she told me. She never wanted kids but...let's just say sex wasn't something she had a choice over. By the time I was ten, I'd lost count of the number of mornings I'd walked into the kitchen and found her passed out on the floor, blood all over her. But he'd never touched me. Had never raised a finger to me."

"But that changed."

She raised her gaze to his, quirking one side of her mouth. "One night he was crazier than usual, and when I tried to help my mom get to the bathroom once he'd finished punching her, he hit me." She paused, clenching her jaw. "More than a few times. I don't remember much, but I do remember hearing my mother scream at him that if he ever touched me again, she'd kill him."

She stopped, taking a few deep breaths.

Sawyer watched her fidget, wondering why in the hell he'd never asked her about her family before. "I'm assuming your father didn't heed your mother's warning."

"Everything was quiet for a while. I guess my dad believed her because he didn't hit me again...until the day he lost his job. He went on some bender, got drunker than usual, and came home swinging. I hid in my bedroom but..."

"But he found you."

She laughed, though it was hollow. "Not too many places to hide. All I remember is him pinning me to the bed, slapping me, ripping at my clothes, calling me a worthless whore, when my mother appeared behind him. She lifted her arm and that was it. I don't know how many times she stabbed him. I suppose until he stopped moving. Sometimes I look in the mirror and still see all that blood."

She stopped and stared at her hands. Something twisted in Sawyer's gut and he didn't know whether to hold her or punch a hole in the wall.

He reached for her hands, thankful when she didn't pull away. "Did she ever try to leave him?"

Her shoulders hunched more and he knew he wasn't going to like what she said next.

"Not once. She'd grown up believing in the sanctity of marriage, and truly believed it was a sin to leave him."

"Makes you wonder why she agreed to marry him in the first place, though I suppose he didn't start hitting her until after they were married."

Mallory shook her head, pulling her hands free as she stood up and walked to the fireplace centred on the far wall. "Oh, no. She knew the kind of man he was. But…"

"But what? Surely she didn't think she could change him?"

She looked over at him, pain clear in her eyes. "Sawyer…you really don't need to know this."

Her sudden reluctance sent more shivers snaking down his spine, but he wasn't about to let her stop now. "On the contrary. I think this is the part I need to hear the most."

Mallory pursed her lips, looking as if she wanted to be anywhere, but there. She forcefully swallowed, bracing one hand on the mantel. "She didn't have a choice. They'd been dating for a while, but after the first time he hit her, she broke it off. I guess my dad wasn't one to take no for an answer. He arranged a meeting, drugged her and drove to Las Vegas. I don't know what kind of drug he used, or where he took her, or how he even got someone to agree to the ceremony, but when she finally came back to her senses, they were married, and she was damned no matter what she did."

The words struck him as surely as if it'd been a physical blow. He pushed off the bar and stalked across the room, punching the top of the couch as he walked by. God. How had he found the one horror in her past and brought it to life?

He turned back to her, anger and shame fighting for dominance. "Fuck, Mallory. Why the hell didn't you ever tell me this?"

"Don't you think I wanted to? But damn it, Sawyer. It's not the kind of thing that comes up. Besides, would you want to tell everyone about your family if that's all you had to say?"

"I'm not *everyone*, and you could have just blurted it out one night. Fuck!" He stomped around the room again, not sure whether to scream or curse. "That's why you freaked out in the hospital. Damn it, I'm a fucking fool."

"I honestly don't remember anything that happened the day of the stabbing, or what followed at the hospital before you left."

"Well, I remember and I can assure you, you weren't pleased. In fact, you were terrified."

He sighed and finally sank down on the sofa, palming his head in his hands. The cushion dipped beside him and her small hand touched his thigh. He turned his head, knowing there was more to say but unable to get any of the words out.

She patted his thigh once before standing again. "I'm sorry I didn't tell you. You're right. You deserved to know."

He leant back, holding her gaze. "Just tell me this. With everything that happened to your mother, why didn't you get our marriage annulled or petition for a divorce? Hell, after the way you reacted, I would have given you either."

Her expression sobered as her lips pulled tight. "How do you divorce the only man you know you'll ever love? You were the one, Sawyer." She paused, looking as if she wasn't sure whether to continue or not. Then she sighed, smiling at him again. "You still are. I couldn't, so I just waited for you to take the initiative, but you never did either and…" She took a few steps back, crossing her arms on her chest. "I'm sorry I woke you. But you really should try to get some sleep. One of us should be coherent tomorrow, and I seriously doubt it'll be me. I'll watch some television until I drift off. The nightmares don't usually come back."

She headed for the other end of the room when he vaulted off the couch, dashing across the room and pinning her to the wall before she could do more than gasp. Her chest pressed against his as her breath came in heavy pants, her lips dangerously close to his. He trapped her between his arms, keeping them on either side of her head as he lowered his face, brushing his mouth across hers.

"Do you honestly think I'm going back to bed after a confession like that? You know me better than that, darling. And considering we're still legally married…I don't see any reason I shouldn't take you to bed." He nipped at her lower lip this time, smiling at the raw rasp that rumbled between them. "Tell me you don't want this, and I'll walk away. For good this time."

She drew a shaky breath, licking her lip when he released it. Her gaze searched his face before a small smile lifted the edges of her mouth. "I can't do that. It'd be a lie."

"In that case, I suggest you take a deep breath, because it's about time we consummated this marriage."

Chapter Four

Sawyer gave her just enough time to anticipate his move before leaning forward and claiming her mouth. Her lips moulded to his, soft and smooth, as he savoured the feel of her skin against his. He didn't rush, despite the urgent need throbbing through him, making his cock feel like a brand against his stomach. But after everything he'd heard, he knew she needed something more than a hot fuck against the wall.

Mallory eased in his arms, opening her mouth on a gentle sigh. He took her unspoken invitation and slipped his tongue inside, tasting the heady flavour of whisky mixed with a familiar tang that was unmistakably hers. She moaned, and he deepened the kiss, sliding one hand off the wall and behind her head, while his other hand curled around her back, pulling her tight to him. She didn't fight his possession, but countered it, wrapping one hand around his neck as the other fisted his briefs, anchoring his groin to hers.

He accepted her challenge, grinding his cock against her pussy, revelling in her breathy gasp. She let her head fall back against the wall when he finally released her, looking at him through half-lidded eyes. Her lips glistened in the pale moonlight, slightly swollen from his kisses, while a delightful blush coloured her cheeks. Her gaze dropped to his crotch, and she licked her lips as his shaft pulsed against the thin fabric of his shorts, tenting the material with its weight.

She looked up at him, raising an eyebrow in question. The simple act flared the head of his penis and he had to squeeze his muscles to keep from creaming his shorts. Damn, she wanted to suck him off, and while his cock wholeheartedly agreed, he knew his need was too raw to allow her that pleasure.

He leaned in, licking her bottom lip before planting a gentle kiss on the corner of her mouth. "As much as I'd love to watch those pretty lips stretch around me, I'm afraid I have other plans." He chuckled when she pouted at him. "Don't worry, darling. You'll get your turn, but first…"

He kissed her again, harder, more demanding. She fought for control, not fully submitting until he grabbed the thin strap on her nightie and tugged it down her arm. She gasped and released his mouth, focusing on his eyes as he repeated the action on the other side, pushing the straps lower until the entire piece fell in a heap at her feet.

He looked down her body, groaning at the pretty pink vee that beckoned to him in the moonlight. She still kept herself bare, and the thought of feeling that supple skin beneath his tongue suddenly became paramount.

"Fuck. You're so damn beautiful." He grabbed both of her hands and pressed them against the wall. "You'd be wise to keep them there."

She opened her mouth in response, but he silenced her with a possessive kiss. Then he slowly sank to his knees, looking up her body at her breasts. They were perky and firm, about the size of his hand. Her nipples had beaded into tiny buds, pointing straight out as if begging him to taste them. He obliged, taking one tight nub between his forefinger and thumb as his mouth descended on the other. A harsh cry lit the air as he rolled the bud between his fingers, working the other with his tongue and teeth. Her body squirmed against him, the subtle scent of her arousal wafting up from between her legs.

He smiled and released her nipple, moving to the other side, tormenting it with the same slow teasing. He heard her fingernails scratch at the wall and knew she was close to disregarding his warning and spearing her fingers through his hair as she tried to move him to where she needed him most.

"Goddamn, Sawyer. It's been two years. Please don't tease me."

He kissed her nipple and inched back, meeting her gaze from between her breasts. Her face was shadowed in the muted light, but he could see the urgency in her eyes. His chest clenched around the thought that she'd waited for him—held their vows sacred though she couldn't even remember them—and he knew he'd move heaven and earth to please her.

"As you wish. Spread your legs and let me get a better look at you."

She sucked the corner of her top lip into her mouth, looking as if she was considering his request, before slowly shifting her legs apart, baring herself to his gaze. He smiled up at her, dropping open-mouthed kisses along her ribs as he moved down her body. Her scar passed below his tongue, the slightly raised skin gaining his attention. He eased back, lifting his fingers to lightly graze the length of it. Mallory's breath hitched and she reached for his hand, but he brushed her away, intent on showing her how lucky he felt to have this second chance. How strong she'd been to stay alive.

"I died a thousand times those first few days. God, when I think—"

"Don't. Don't think. Just love me."

He glanced up at her, smiling at the passion shining in her eyes. "You're right. There'll be time to *discuss* your reckless behaviour later. But first things first."

He gave the mark one final kiss, pushing away the panicky feeling as he inched down her body again, circling her belly button before moving to the top of her mound. The sweet scent of her musk permeated his senses and he couldn't stop from darting his tongue out and swiping it through her slit.

Her strangled cry sounded above him, muffled only by the pounding of his blood in his ears. He still wasn't certain how he'd gone from unwanted asshole to loving husband in what felt like a heartbeat, but he wasn't going to waste this chance. And by the time he was finished, the only words that would come to her mind were 'I do' and 'again'.

He backed away slightly, watching her pretty nether lips quiver at his departure. They glistened with her juice, and he knew she was close to climaxing.

"Damn, darling. I've only just started and you look desperate."

"You're looking pretty anxious yourself, baby. Or are you planning on pounding some nails in with that rod?"

"Naughty talk. And certainly not the kind that will get you fucked."

"Sawyer."

He chuckled at the authority in her voice, so raw and husky he'd barely understood his name. He leant forward, tasting her again, moaning at the earthy tang of her and how her voice carried across the room. "That's it. Fight it."

Her thighs trembled as he stroked his tongue from her cleft to her nub, flicking the tip across her tightly knotted nerves. She screamed this time, tilting her hips to increase the pressure. He thought about moving with her, keeping his touch light, but he could tell by the way her muscles quivered, she was too far gone for more teasing.

Next time, he told himself, slipping a finger into her crease and sinking just the tip inside her. Her walls clenched on the gentle intrusion, clamping around his skin as if desperate for more. He relented, easing his finger deeper until his palm cupped her flesh and he was fully inside her.

She bucked against him, trying to set up some kind of rhythm. He followed her lead, gliding his finger in and out of her grasping channel, feeling her walls give and contract around his penetration.

"So tight. It feels amazing."

She whimpered something incoherent, spreading her thighs more as her knees started to tremble. He reached one of his hands under her ass, holding her up as he quickened his pace, using two fingers to part her tender folds. She called his name, and he moved his tongue back to her clit, lapping at it as he claimed her sex. Her orgasm loomed closer, marked by the increase in her arousal and the urgent gasps from low in her throat. He pumped her faster, matching the pace with the flick of his tongue. When her thighs stiffened, her breath releasing in a painful rasp, he suckled her clit into his mouth, driving his fingers hard and deep into her sex.

Her sharp intake of breath was followed by a keening wail as her pussy convulsed, sending tiny tremors coursing through his body as she climaxed around him. Liquid heat coated his tongue as he tasted her release, hot and sweet. He heard her gasp in more air as her strength finally waned, her body suspended only by his hand on her ass and one of her feet wedged against his knee. He smiled, letting her feel the movement on her bare lips, before slowly gaining his feet. Her head had lolled against the wall again and her eyes were squeezed shut, but he grinned when he saw she'd kept her hands fisted at her side like he'd instructed.

Sawyer shucked his briefs, tossing them over his shoulder as he pressed his body tight to hers, cupping one hand under her right thigh. Her eyelids flew open as his cock brushed across her mound, tempting her opening with the promise of his shaft sliding deep inside her. She followed his lead, wrapping first one leg, then the other, around the small of his back, relying on the strength in his arms braced below her buttocks to hold her up. He shifted his weight, lodging his cock an inch inside her.

Mallory moaned, encircling his neck with her arms as she tilted her groin, taking him slightly deeper. Sawyer growled against her neck, nipping at the corded muscles as he arched back then drove forward, claiming her passage in one hard stroke.

"God. Yes."

Her voice echoed in his head as his chin fell forward, resting on her shoulder as he dragged his shaft through her tight folds, stopping with just the tip inside her. She whispered his name, begging him this time, and he thrust again, sinking deep as his balls slapped her ass.

"Bloody hell, darling. You're so fucking tight. Too tight. Damn..."

His words morphed into grunts and groans as his need took over, and he fucked her hard against the wall, using his weight and his arms to hold her up as he pounded into her, gritting his teeth against the exquisite clench of her pussy along his shaft. Every thrust pushed the head deep in her channel, while every retreat rippled the length of his cock as her walls fluttered around him. Pleasure and pain streaked along his spine, threatening to unhinge him with every stroke.

Mallory cried out, her head banging against the wall as he surged deep, igniting a cascade effect inside her. Her channel clamped down hard on his shaft, while her walls contracted in rhythmic pulses, coating his cock with her slippery cream. He felt her entire body shatter around him, and he gave in to the rush of fire that pooled in his balls before erupting down his shaft, triggering a release that left him sagging in her arms. Pulse after pulse of his seed purged from the tip, and by the time the dizzying array of black spots cleared from his vision, he could feel their combined release wet against his sac.

It occurred to him that they hadn't used protection, not that he was concerned about catching anything. And she'd always taken the pill before, but...

Sawyer pressed his forehead against hers, drinking in the heady scent of their sex. Sweet and spicy, it was the perfect mixture of love and lust, and he knew he'd never tire of it. He took a deep breath, pushing away his worries. Somehow the thought of her pregnant with his child didn't scare him as it had before, and he found himself smiling at the notion as he slowly eased back, allowing her legs to slip off his hips as her feet touched the wooden floor. He held back a disgruntled chuckle when he realised he'd done exactly what he'd told himself not to — fucked her hard against the wall, though from the way she sagged against him, he didn't think she cared. Her body shook with subtle aftershocks as he reluctantly pulled his weakening erection from her tight clasp.

"Don't go."

The words were nothing more than a breath of air across his neck, but he felt the weight of them down to his toes. He kissed her mouth, coaxing her gaze up to his. "God, you're amazing. And now that we've gotten the sex out of the way, I can make love to you."

Her eyes widened as he scooped her up and headed for the bedroom. While he'd enjoyed the rawness of their fuck against the wall, now he needed something deeper — something pure. Mallory didn't speak. She just wrapped her arms around his neck, peppering kisses along his jaw as he kicked open her door, then toed it shut, striding confidently to the bed. Their gazes clashed as he stopped at the edge and gently lowered her onto the soft sheets.

He drew his fingers along her jaw, overwhelmed by the sheer beauty of her. Dark, wavy hair framed her oval face, highlighting the pale tones in her skin. Her blue eyes sparkled like sunlight on the water, and her silky skin gleamed with a light sheen of sweat.

He smiled as he twirled a few errant strands of hair around his fingers, remembering his earlier wish to gather it in his hands as he claimed her mouth. "Are you sure you're up for another round?"

She smirked at him, her gaze dropping to his groin. Though he was far from fully erect, already he could feel his cock lengthening against his thighs, hardening from the sheer lust shining in her eyes.

"You promised you'd make love to me. I'd hate to have to wrestle you into submission."

He chuckled at her warning, moving forward to capture her mouth in his as his hand fisted her hair. It was even better than he'd envisioned. He dropped a kiss on her nose when he finally pulled back, loving how her eyelids fluttered a few times before opening.

"If you're trying to scare me, you'll have to pick something that doesn't equate to a fantasy. 'Cause rolling around on the bed with you is hardly the stuff of nightmares."

"Just because you're bigger than me—"

He captured the rest of her words in his mouth as he lunged forward, taking them both down on the bed. Mallory squirmed beneath him, but only enough to get her legs out from underneath him before wrapping them around his hips again. She pressed her heels into the small of his back, seating him snugly between her thighs.

Sawyer ravaged her mouth, alternating between plunging his tongue deep and tasting the salty perfection of her skin as he covered her jaw with open-mouthed kisses. She returned the same, moaning his name as she tried to rub every inch of her body against his. For a moment, he worried his weight was squishing her into the bed, but the concern vanished when she tilted her hips and took the first thick inch of him inside her.

He stopped, clenching his teeth as he closed his eyes and staved off the riot of sensations coursing through him. Her lips brushed the column of his throat, making their way slowly towards his shoulder. A scrape of her teeth jerked his hips, plunging his cock deeper.

"Wench. You did that on purpose."

She smiled at him when he looked down at her, her eyelids briefly closing as a ripple shivered through her. He could feel every reaction of her body as it joined with his, from the pooling of hot juices along his shaft to the thrashing pulse of her heart as it thundered against his chest.

"I warned you I'd wrestle you into submission."

"Fuck, if this is your idea of wrestling, I'll build us a permanent ring."

She laughed, a musical sound that made his mouth curl into a smile and his heart squeeze tight in his chest. He took a deep breath, slipping his arms underneath her shoulders as he gathered her close, lowering his face until it hovered inches above hers. He stared into her eyes, daring her to look away as he slowly sank inside her passage, feeling every inch of her body give as he surged deeper, stopping when his sac slapped her ass.

"Damn." He moaned, fighting to keep his gaze on hers.

"Sawyer."

Her voice was a combination of need and love and he bent lower as he brushed his lips over hers, wanting her to feel every emotion roiling inside him. Her hands palmed his back, tracing his muscles as he eased his aching cock out of her before thrusting it back in. Her head pushed into the mattress, exposing the long line of her neck.

He kissed the soft spot on her shoulder, nipping at the hollow. "Mallory."

Her eyelids opened at the whispered rasp of her name and the look she gave him stopped his heart. She'd never shown him that much of herself, granting him access to every recess of her heart. He could feel her love for him in the way she speared her fingers through his hair, drawing him down for another soul-searing kiss.

He put all his love for her into that one kiss, wanting her to realise her trust hadn't been misplaced. A soft sob drifted past his ear and he drew back, watching a wash of tears caress her cheek. He smiled, brushing them away with the pad of his thumb. He'd never seen her cry before, and knowing he'd pushed her past her limits humbled him.

"That's it, darling. Don't hold back. Give me everything."

He moved faster, wanting to hear her scream his name again as she broke. Her breathing increased, the rapid pants matching the frenzied movement of his hips as he claimed her pussy, plunging deep then pulling back, keeping just the crown inside her. His name rose like a prayer from her lips as her eyes rolled shut and her head pressed back. He rode her hard, wishing he could go slower but too lost in the soft press of her sex and the wet sound of his balls slapping her butt. Her juice coated his shaft, heating his way, driving him forward. The tell-tale fire blazed a path down his spine, and he knew he wouldn't last much longer.

Sawyer clenched his jaw, determined to hold off until she'd creamed his cock again. He shifted his body, angling his hips higher, knowing the new position would rub his pelvis across her clit.

"God. Yes. Now, now, now."

Her voice filled the room, the desperate plea unhinging his control. He lowered his head, whispering her name against the shell of her ear as he slammed into her, all hope of gentleness gone. She moved with him, chanting his name as her body tensed, then broke, her shattered cry drowning out the frantic beating of his heart. He kept moving, claiming her channel over and over until the feeling overwhelmed him and he came, shooting his release deep inside her. His muscles clenched, holding him rigid above her as he emptied himself, feeling as if she'd consumed his very soul.

Her ragged gasp raked across his jaw and he lowered his head, mixing his breath with hers. Thoughts and words merged into one, and all he could do was lie there, holding her with the intention of never letting go. A warm wash of tears touched his skin, and he eased back just enough to gaze into her eyes. Love and something deeper gleamed back at him, and he smiled as he brushed one side of her cheek.

"I'm praying these are a result of my mastery in the bedroom, and not because you regret what just happened."

She swallowed hard, shaking her head as she nuzzled the palm of his hand. "I'm just…"

Her words morphed into a sigh, and he nodded. Hell, he felt as raw as she looked and was surprised he had the clarity to remember his own name.

He dipped down, claiming her mouth in a soft, sensuous kiss. Her fingers teased the back of his neck before shifting down and cupping each side of his face. She held his gaze, baring her soul to him before whispering his name again and kissing his forehead.

His strength waned and he moved to one side, wondering whether to pull her onto his chest or spoon against her ass when worry creased her brow and she grabbed his arm, holding him close.

"Please don't leave."

Her voice barely registered, but there was no mistaking the fear laced within it. He furrowed his brow, wondering why she thought he'd want to be anywhere other than beside her in the bed.

He reached for her, running his fingers through her hair. "I'm not going anywhere tonight. But I should grab a cloth and clean you up before you pass out on me. Okay?"

She worried her bottom lip for a moment, the unconscious hesitation increasing his concern, before she smiled and released his arm, watching him as he pushed off the bed and sauntered to the bathroom. He glanced back at her as he walked through, making sure she knew he had every intention of returning as promised. He went to the cupboard and opened the door, grabbing a small cloth off the shelf. He glanced in the mirror as he turned on the tap, letting it run until the water felt warm beneath his fingertips. A small mark just above his collarbone drew his attention and he smiled at the hickey marring his skin. Damn, she was feisty.

He gave the blemish a quick rinse then cleaned his shaft, revelling in the combined scent of their sex as he rinsed the cloth and headed for the door. Her gaze followed him as he moved back to the bed, dipping the mattress with his weight. She didn't speak as he gently parted her thighs, dabbing the warm material along her cleft, removing the evidence of their torrid lovemaking. Part of him pouted at the act, wanting nothing more than to see his cum dripping from her pussy, showing the world she was his. But the sensible side of him knew she wouldn't get a restful sleep if he left her sticky and wet. And right now, her comfort was all he could think about.

He bathed her clit. A subtle shiver shuddered through her, and he couldn't help but smile in smug victory. Just a hint of his touch and she'd had another small orgasm.

"You're dangerous, darling. No wonder Cole wants you as his partner."

She snorted. "Cole's never fucked me against the wall."

"And it's a damn good thing 'cause I'd hate to have to kill the man."

She shook her head in feigned annoyance as he climbed over her, trailing his hand up her hip and across her stomach, finally settling it in the soft valley of her breasts. The steady thrum of her heart vibrated his fingertips and he sighed as he snuggled her close, inhaling the scent of floral soap and cocoanut shampoo.

"Now try to get some sleep. I'll keep you safe."

Mallory kissed his arm and burrowed closer, staying strangely quiet as she relaxed against him, her breath quickly deepening as she gave in to the fatigue he'd seen creasing her brow and bunching her shoulders. He lay there for several minutes, holding her while she slept, rerunning the events of the night in his head. Though he'd seduced her into bed, he had a strange feeling he was far from being a permanent fixture in her life. She'd given him everything...bared a part of her he'd never seen before, but even so, he felt as if she was holding back. As if there was still something wedged between them, threatening to undo all he'd strived to achieve tonight.

He sighed, closing his eyes as he listened to her breathe, the soft, muffled sound lulling him into a hazy fog. He'd worry about everything tomorrow, when some of his blood had returned to his brain. When every waking thought wasn't shaded in the colour of her skin and how it contrasted perfectly with his.

He heard himself laugh. Who was he kidding? The day she didn't occupy his every thought was the day he died, pure and simple. And he had absolutely no intentions of dying before spending the next fifty years loving her.

Chapter Five

Mallory prised her eyelids apart, squinting against the throbbing pain beating in her head, as a hand shook her shoulder, preventing her from succumbing to the desire to simply roll over and snuggle beneath the covers. She tried to focus, dragging her gaze upwards until it settled on Sawyer's face. He gave her a stunning smile that fluttered her stomach and ignited a new wave of pain.

She groaned, squeezing her temples as she rolled, letting her head fall back on the bed. "What time is it?"

"Seven-thirty. Here, take these."

He nudged her with his hand and she shifted her gaze just enough to see the pills and glass in his hands.

She peered at him. "What are those?"

"Spanish fly. What the hell do you think they are? Motrin. Now take them before those bongos in your head get any louder."

She scowled at him, but took the pills, downing them with a gulp of water. "How did you know?"

He snorted, his ass crowding the space beside her. "You downed four shots of whisky in the space of a heartbeat last night—all on an empty stomach. It doesn't take a neurosurgeon to figure out you might feel like shit this morning." His gave travelled down the length of her body, pausing at her hips. "Other than the headache, you feeling okay?"

"If you're asking me if I can still walk after your, how did you put it, 'mastery in the bedroom', it'll be tricky, but I think I'll manage." She rolled her eyes at the smug look of satisfaction on his face. "Please tell me Cole isn't here yet."

"No. I called him ten minutes ago, just to be sure he wasn't in the habit of dropping by to see if you'd made it through another night. Told him we'd meet him at the office." He raised a brow. "But by your comment, I assume he usually does? Stop by?"

"Most days. But I told you. It was never like that. He's just a nice guy who's overly paranoid I don't know how to take care of myself."

"And rightly so. That milk in your fridge could be used as chemical warfare. Hell, you don't even have any bread."

She shrugged, regretting the action when her head responded with a stab of pain. "I haven't been home much."

"Apparently." He sighed, patting her hip. "You know, I'm sure you have more than your fair share of sick days. Cole and I can handle things today if you'd rather stay here and catch up on some sleep."

Mallory closed her eyes, considering his offer, but she knew she couldn't accept. An entire day of sitting around, rehashing everything she'd confessed to Sawyer, wouldn't help her feel better. Hell, after the night they'd shared, it'd only ratchet up her stress.

She'd opened up to him, more than she'd ever planned to, and she wasn't quite sure how she felt about it. She pried her eyelids apart again, her chest tightening at the concerned look in his eyes. Damn, how was she supposed to act casual when he made his feelings so obvious?

"Thanks, but I'll be fine." She smiled at his slight frown. "Besides, what fun is spending the day in bed if you're not in it with me?"

Lust flashed in his eyes and he leant forward, placing a hand on either side of her shoulders. "Careful, darling, or I might just develop a serious case of 'fuck it' and have to take you up on your offer." His gaze dropped to her chest. He'd always been a breast guy, though he'd spent his fair share of time licking her pussy last night.

The memory had her squirming beneath the sheet, the ghostly feel of his tongue on her clit pooling a fresh wave of moisture along her slit. He must have sensed her increased arousal. He tsked at her and yanked off the cover, his hand going to the aching nub between her legs.

"Damn, Mal, you're fucking soaking."

She could only grunt her reply, his talented fingers teasing her nerves as they danced through her folds, spreading her liquid heat along the length of her cleft. But just as he reached her sex, tempting it with a hint of penetration, he pulled back and jumped to his feet, towering over her with a feral look in his eyes.

"Sawyer…"

Her words keened into a startled gasp as he slipped his hands under her, lifting her from the bed and shuffling her into his arms.

He smiled, dropping a kiss on her open mouth before heading across the room. "Shower. Now."

The firm tone in his voice stopped any protest she might have made and she knew he was on the verge of fucking her against the wall again, or on the counter, hell, maybe the floor. She held on, loving the feel of being in his arms. Despite everything she'd told herself, about how strong she was and how she didn't need anyone's protection, she loved how he always made her feel safe.

The truth of the statement tugged at her subconscious, threatening to unleash something she suspected was better left buried. Just talking about her childhood had opened a raw wound, and she was more than aware that nothing good would come from dwelling on those memories.

Sawyer marched them into the bathroom, easing her down when he reached the shower. He didn't wait for her to ask to undress him, simply removed his briefs and left them lying forgotten on the floor. He opened the glass door, turning on the water before extending his hand and gently holding hers as he pulled her inside.

She stepped in after him, gasping when he growled and pinned her against the tiled wall. The cold porcelain bit into her skin, surpassed only by the heat of his body as he snugged his chest against hers, the long length of his cock pressing into the slight hollow beside her hip.

He took a deep breath, making the muscle in his jaw twitch as he rested his forehead against hers. It was a familiar move, one he made when he struggled to come to grips with his control. But she didn't care about his control. He seemed to think she needed gentle, tame. What she wanted was Sawyer, raw, hungry, almost brutal in his desire, as he took her hot and hard against any convenient surface.

She heard him exhale a long, slow breath as he eased back, watching her amidst a spray of water. She smiled and pushed him away slightly, wanting a chance to finally get a good, hard look at him. Though she'd felt every inch of him rock against her last night, she hadn't had near enough time to touch and taste as she longed to. Sawyer furrowed his brow as he took a step back, uncertainty creasing his forehead.

Mallory allowed her gaze to run the length of his body. "Damn. You're one fine-looking man."

She held up her hand, shaking her index finger at him when he smiled and tried to press forward.

"Not this time, baby. I believe it's my turn."

He held her gaze as she ran her fingers across his chest, tracing each band of muscle, watching as they twitched beneath the pads of her fingers. He looked slightly larger than she remembered and she could only guess he'd been hitting the gym pretty hard. She moved forward, dipping her mouth to his skin, tasting the spicy combination of water and man. He cursed under his breath as she followed the path of her fingers with her tongue, gently probing every dip and plane on his torso. It wasn't until his hands raked through her hair, pulling the wet strands off her face that she sank to her knees, holding her breath as she stopped level with his cock.

"Mallory. Darling. I'm not sure I can handle the feel of that wicked mouth of yours on my cock right now."

She glanced up at him, allowing one finger to tease the tip of his shaft. "Are you asking me not to give you a blowjob? 'Cause as I recall, you quite enjoyed coming in my mouth."

"Fuck!"

His head fell back on the tiles as she bent forward and licked the hood of his shaft, keeping her tongue flat to cover as much of his skin as possible. The crown flared beneath her touch, beading a drop of pre-cum on the slit. She glanced up at him. Somehow he'd managed to keep his head pressed against the wall, but still maintain eye contact, his blue eyes nearly black with desire. She held his gaze and poked out her tongue again, licking away the drop, humming at the unique flavour of him. It was spicy and salty and just the feel of his slippery fluid on her tongue eased a wave of moisture down her slit.

"Damn, darling. You look so fucking hot with my cock in your hand, your mouth watering just to taste it." He nodded at her. "Open your knees. Let me see how wet sucking me gets you."

She raised an eyebrow, silently reminding him this was her seduction, but relented and slid her thighs apart, baring her clit to the humid air. Despite the temperature, her body cooled and she flexed her muscles, making the tiny hood flutter. His harsh moan told her the subtle action hadn't gone unnoticed.

She grinned again, holding his shaft even with her mouth as she parted her lips and slowly took him inside, taking him deep to the back of her throat. Sawyer made a garbled choking sound as his hands tightened in her hair. She embraced the slight sting, easing him out only to circle his head with her tongue before engulfing him again.

"So hot and wet. God, your mouth feels so good."

His hips tilted, and he thrust forward, the slight hesitation making her smile. He was trying to let her lead, but the sheer magnitude of his need was slowly taking control. She didn't stop him, merely angling her head a bit to accommodate his movements. They started off slow, just a small roll of his hips, but then built in intensity until all restraint vanished and he fucked her mouth like he'd taken her against the wall the previous night.

Mallory moved with him, pumping his cock as she sucked the head, swallowing every drop of fluid that eased from the slit. His shaft pulsed again, and his balls tightened beneath her hand. She closed her eyes, readying herself for that one moment when he allowed himself to be vulnerable. The one time she truly held the power. But just as his cock swelled in her mouth, he stopped, pulling himself free.

"No. Sawyer. Please."

He stopped her protest by lifting her up and trapping her against the wall, his body squishing hers. One thigh wedged between her legs, and she didn't hesitate from rubbing herself on him, sending jolts of pleasure straight to her core.

He reached up and palmed her chin, forcing her to look at him. "As much as I want to come in your mouth, I don't think I'll be ready again before we have to leave. And there's no goddamn way I'm leaving here without feeling you come around my cock one more time."

"But..."

Her voice became a moan of ecstasy as he cupped her thighs, lifting her up and hilting himself inside her. Water splashed across her face as he pulled back, his broad shoulders deflecting the spray, covering them with a mist of rain. He rammed deep again, making her scream. Her nails dug into his back, but she couldn't stop, couldn't breathe past the frantic thrust of his shaft, the heavy rasp of his breath past her ear as he pressed his forehead to the wall beside her and let go.

His movements became a blur of skin and white tile as he claimed her sex, pushing her from one orgasm into another. She heard herself beg, plead with him for just one more release, knowing when it came she'd be lucky to survive it. He moved his head, capturing her mouth in his as he slammed home one more time, sending them both into climax.

The warm rush of his seed inflamed her already swollen tissues, drawing the orgasm out until all she could do was bow her head against his as her strength drained from her body. She did her best to keep her arms looped around his neck, but when he finally eased his hold, allowing her feet to touch the floor, she collapsed against him, knowing he'd somehow keep her upright.

Sawyer whispered soothing words in her ear as his hands swirled across her body, leaving a trail of suds behind. He worked his way downward, smiling at her hushed moan before angling them under the spray and rinsing off the soap. Their gazes clashed as he shut off the water and elbowed open the glass door, grabbing two towels. His gaze never left hers as he wrapped the fluffy terry around her, slinging his across his shoulder as he carried her out. He didn't stop until they'd reached the bedroom and he'd placed her in front of a chair. She stumbled onto it, thankful she didn't have to hold herself up as her knees buckled. Sawyer knelt down in front of her, laying his head across her thighs. Something shifted inside her as she stroked her hands through his hair, wishing they could spend the day in bed, but knowing the fragile atmosphere would shatter all too soon.

A hesitant smile touched her lips. Best start to her day in a long time. She could only hope it didn't bite her in the ass later.

* * * *

"Bloody hell."

Mallory looked over at Cole, watching him slam his fist on the desk. The man had become more frustrated every day they'd worked on the new case, and after a week, she was surprised his desk didn't have a dent across the surface.

She leant back in her chair. "Something on your mind, Cole?"

He cursed again, sneering at the box on his desk before finally meeting her gaze. "I've been through every box of evidence a dozen times this past week. Whoever got Davies' samples didn't get it from the old files. Nothing's missing — not a vial, a swab, not so much as a fucking Band-Aid."

An unsettled lump formed in her throat as she nodded, trying not to think about the implications of his statement. That'd been their first assumption — that whoever was trying to make it look like Davies' work had simply stolen evidence from the previous cases. Ruling that out left few options, all of them more disturbing than the last one.

She ran her fingers through her hair, thankful she'd left it down today, not that she'd had a choice. Though they'd been keeping their encounters limited to nighttime hours, Sawyer had decided to surprise her in the bathroom this morning after running out for coffee and had fucked her senseless from behind while she was bent over the counter. And despite her assurances that all was well, Cole had decided to resume his ritual of dropping by the house every morning and had already been ringing the doorbell by the time Sawyer had shouted her name, coming inside her with one last strong thrust.

She fought the smile that threatened, knowing now wasn't the time or the place for it. She refocused on Cole. "We knew that might be the case. It just means that the samples must have been collected after he was incarcerated. At least that narrows down the possible suspects."

"Yeah, to cops and guards and fucking lawyers." Cole grunted. "No one visited the bastard, Mal. You know that as well as I do. So that means either the guy's got more lives than a damn cat and more magic than *Houdini*, or our killer is someone in the system."

"Sick, but a badge doesn't make you a saint, buddy."

"Saint? I'd settle for somewhere close to normal."

Mallory chuckled, pushing to her feet as she stretched her arms. Her muscles protested the movement, reminding her of how 'used' they felt, despite the fact she hadn't been to the gym since Sawyer's arrival.

A smug smile curved her lips and she looked away, afraid Cole would recognise the love-sick expression on her face. She mumbled something about coffee and headed for the lounge, hoping the break would clear her thoughts, and get Sawyer the hell out of them before he came back from grabbing them all a burger.

She walked into the room and headed for the sink, rinsing her mug before pouring herself another cup. No wonder she didn't get any sleep. Between Sawyer making love to her for half the night and the gallon of caffeine she had ingested, it was a miracle she functioned at all.

A hand settled on her shoulder and she gasped, nearly dropping her coffee as she spun around, spilling half of it on the floor. Director Henderson grimaced, handing her some napkins as she cursed and bent down to clean up the mess.

"Sorry, Mallory. I didn't mean to startle you."

She sighed, standing up and tossing the soaked serviettes in the garbage. "I damn near turned around swinging, Don."

He flashed her a smile. "Then I'll consider a splash of putrid coffee a godsend."

"You're here late."

He scowled at her as he grabbed a cloth and dabbed the small stain on the front of his shirt. "You should talk. The three of you look like zombies. Are any of you getting any sleep?"

She felt a hot blush creep into her cheeks and turned away, using the coffee machine as a convenient excuse. God help her if he only knew how she was spending her nights. "Some."

He cleared his throat, looking at her with that arrogant grin when she dared to glance at him over her shoulder.

She huffed. "A little. But need I remind you that you did instruct us to put all of our resources into finding this creep."

"Resources, yes. Digging yourselves early graves, however…"

She sighed, feeling the inklings of guilt tease her conscience, though she knew it wasn't warranted. Even if Sawyer wasn't making love to her for half the night, the nightmares would've taken his place.

Don released a loud breath, leaning against the counter beside her. "I suppose I do owe you an apology."

She arched a brow. "For what?"

"For not killing Sawyer. You've been a model agent where he's concerned."

Another flash of heat burnt her cheeks. Model agent? Though she wasn't certain of the exact criteria, she was pretty damn sure stripping the man naked and begging him to fuck her against the wall until he shouted her name as he creamed her pussy wasn't part of the equation. She fought the grin tugging at her lips. "The case isn't over, Don. Don't thank me, yet. I still have time to be a complete embarrassment to the Bureau."

Emphasis on bare and ass.

He studied her then shook his head. "I'll give you the benefit of the doubt for now. Besides, Cole tells me you've allowed Sawyer to sleep in your spare room all week. Doesn't sound like the workings of a killer to me."

"On the contrary, it gives me more time to properly plot his murder."

The smile he gave her said all she needed to know. Damn, she was going to have to talk to Cole about improving his poker face.

Don walked over to the doorway, stopping at the threshold. "As long as you strangle the man on your own time..." He turned then seemed to change his mind, glancing over at her as he hovered half in and half out of the room. "Off the record, Mallory. I gotta know. Did you and Sawyer really get married?"

She couldn't stop the grin from spreading across her face this time as she moved over to him, pausing beside him. "Off the record, I think the real question should be...are we still married?"

His eyes widened in shock before he swore under his breath.

She patted his shoulder, stepping through. "Don't worry, sir, I have no intentions of destroying your plausible deniability."

Mallory was still smiling as she ambled back to her desk, the heady scent of grilled beef gaining her attention. Her stomach growled as she moved in behind Sawyer, thanking him when he handed her a burger and fries. He nodded at her, mumbling something about how she'd eat all of it if she knew what was best for her, before sinking into his chair. Cole already had half the burger devoured and was making headway on the fries by the time she popped one in her mouth, savouring the salty tang on her tongue. It reminded her of the spicy taste of Sawyer's skin when they made love.

Cole looked over at her, chewing on a mouthful of burger. "Hey, you okay? You look flushed."

She felt Sawyer's gaze on her and knew he'd seen through her façade. "It's just the spice on the burger."

Cole gave her a funny look then shrugged, taking another mouthful. She chanced a glance at Sawyer, instantly wishing she hadn't. His eyes had darkened slightly, the promise in them stealing her breath. God, what more could the man do to her that he hadn't done a hundred times in the past couple of nights? Hell, he'd licked her pussy so much she swore she had an imprint of his tongue on her clit.

A hysterical giggle threatened, but she tamped it down, enjoying the brief reprieve as they ate in silence. Somehow they'd managed to maintain a platonic relationship at the office, and not even Cole had questioned her about their living arrangements, though she suspected that was an oversight he'd eventually put right. But until then, they'd play the roles the Bureau expected them to.

She was halfway through her meal when her phone rang. The sharp sound startled her, and she laughed when she jumped in her seat, nearly knocking over her drink. Cole shook his head and nodded at the phone.

She flipped him the bird as she reached for it. "Reeves."

"Hey, Mallory. It's Fisher."

"Goddamn, what now?"

"Nice to talk to you, too. Oh, I'm fine. Thanks for asking."

She sighed, resting her elbow on her desk. "Sorry. You know I love talking to you, but it's seldom good news when you call work on your day off, so out with it. What now?"

"It might not be anything but..."

"But what?"

"You remember Daniel, right?"

Her lips quirked slightly. "Tall, sexy homicide detective you've secretly been dating for three months? Yeah, he comes to mind."

"Shit. How the hell do you know about that?"

"I'm paid to be observant. What's up with Daniel?"

"He's got the damn police scanner going and there's been a number of reports about a suspicious van over on the south side. A couple of units have gone by, but the calls keep coming in even after nothing weird was found, so Dan called dispatch. They're all from the same caller. It's a pay phone, but dispatch has a location."

"Do I want to know where this person is calling from?"

"It's coming from Plymouth Street, Mal...you know, where..."

Mallory felt the blood drain from her face as she glanced up at the guys. Sawyer furrowed his brow while Cole stopped in mid-bite, staring at her as if she'd seen a ghost.

She nodded even though she knew Fisher couldn't see her. "Shit."

"I thought you might see it that way. Again, it could be nothing but—"

"But it's one hell of a coincidence." She released a rough breath. "Thanks. We owe you guys. And hey, do you think Daniel could do us a favour and let the precinct know we're checking it out, just in case some rookie gets anxious? I don't need another trip to the emergency room."

"Will do and Mallory…be careful."

She hung up, a tight feeling closing around her throat. She hadn't been back to that alley since…

"Mallory? You okay?"

Sawyer's voice broke through her haze and she glanced up to see him standing in front of her. Cole was already grabbing his jacket off his chair as he shoved the remains of his dinner aside.

She swung her gaze back at Sawyer, praying she didn't look as scared as she felt. "Fisher said there's a bunch of calls coming in from the same pay phone about a suspicious van, even though patrols have been by. They're coming from Plymouth Street…"

Sawyer's mouth pulled into a tight line as he glanced at Cole over his shoulder. "Could be our guy getting far too cocky. Davies used to call in all of his killings." He turned back to her. "Why don't you let Cole and I check it out? We'll call you if we find anything."

He took two steps before she caught up to him, grabbing his arm as she yanked him back around. "You don't seriously believe I'm going to fall for that, do you?" She waved off his reply. "I'm a big girl, Sawyer. And I'm not about to let some psychotic jackass scare me off by picking a location I'm intimately familiar with. So if going there bothers you, stay put. Otherwise, let's go."

She heard Sawyer curse as she pushed by him, her heart thundering in her chest. Seemed his early prediction was coming true—she could run all she wanted, but they were far from done.

Chapter Six

Rain splattered against the windshield as they pulled over, stopping just shy of the alley. Lightning flashed overhead, illuminating random patches of pavement as Mallory stared at the darkened entrance. Disjointed memories tickled the edge of her consciousness — Sawyer's voice yelling at her, the wail of sirens in the distance, the flicker of lights overhead — nothing concrete but more than enough to persuade her not to dig any deeper.

Sawyer shoved the Jeep into first gear and yanked on the emergency brake, glancing at her before turning to face Cole in the backseat. "If I swing this thing any closer, it could tip someone off, if there's anyone actually in the alleyway. I thought it'd be better to check it out on foot."

Cole unholstered his Glock, checking the chamber. "Sounds like a plan." He glanced at her. "Don't suppose you'd agree to stay here and call for backup if we need it?"

She didn't dignify his question with a reply. Instead, she rolled her eyes and opened the door, stepping onto the sidewalk. Multiple groans sounded behind her, but she ignored them. As much as she didn't relish the thought of revisiting this place, she wasn't about to shy away because of some bad memories.

Icy drops cooled her face as she stalked to the corner of the alley, waiting for Sawyer and Cole to move in behind her. Thunder clapped overhead as a blaze of light flashed across the sky, casting long shadows down the dark corridor. A cat whined in the distance, followed by a hushed scraping sound that nearly got lost in the patter of rain.

Mallory held up her fist as the men neared, cocking her head to get a better bead on the noise. She nodded at them, holding her gun beside her face as she counted to three. As she hit the number, she slipped out, clearing the space with her weapon as the men darted to the other side, angling behind a collection of soggy boxes. A dull thud echoed down the lane, prickling goose bumps along her skin. There was something distinctly eerie about the sound, as if she'd heard it before.

Sawyer motioned ahead and she moved, staying in step with them as they made their way down the alley, keeping to the dark recesses lining the walls on either side. Shadows rippled across the pavement, the lightning making it hard to determine what was solid and what was merely a ghosted reflection from the storm. Metal pieces of fencing and trash flickered with each sporadic flash, giving the alley a disco-tech feel. A muffled grunt stopped them as they neared a junction.

Cole fell in behind her, grabbing her arm as she went to peek around the corner. "I'll go first."

Mallory glared at him, pulling her arm free. "I thought Sawyer was already playing the part of the overprotective Neanderthal, or are you his new sidekick?"

"Bite me, sweetheart. Now back off, or I might choose now to ask you exactly where it is Sawyer's sleeping."

"I'll bite you later. And you already know where he's sleeping. We'll go on three again."

Cole scowled but counted, jumping out with her when he reached three. The alley looked deserted, with nothing more than a couple of dumpsters and some discarded garbage lining the sides. Mallory eased forward, drawn to a dark blur near the end of the lane. Something about it seemed out of place. She kept watching, slowly making her way forward, when a flash of silver gleamed in the darkness.

Mallory dove forward, yelling out a warning as the report of a gun shattered the night. She rolled to her side, firing off three rounds as Cole dashed in beside her. He grabbed her arm and pulled her behind one of the dumpsters. Two more bullets ricocheted off the metal, filling the alley with a resounding twang.

Cole ducked out, firing a shot towards the end of the road, before slipping back in. "Did you get a look at the guy?"

Mallory shook her head, glancing over at Sawyer. He'd taken cover behind the discarded hood of a car, and she wondered how long he could stay safe there. She nodded towards them, but he shook his head, wincing when another shot hit the pavement not far from his shoulder.

"Damn it, what the hell is Sawyer doing? And no, I didn't get a look at the guy. Shit, Cole, it's black as ass down here."

"Your ass or mine? Because I'm pretty damn certain your ass is pearly white."

Mallory could only sigh. The man was impossible. She looked over at Sawyer, reading his intentions by the way he tensed his body. She waved at him to stop, but he shook his head, pointing at the end of the alley.

"Goddamn. Sawyer is going to pull a fucking John Wayne." She turned to Cole. "Be ready to cover me."

"Cover you? Are you crazy? We have no idea what we're up against."

"Tell that to Sawyer."

Cole huffed, glancing at the other man. "I take back anything I ever said. You two are a perfect match. You both should be committed." He pressed closer to her back. "I've got you. Just stick to the shadows and stay close to Sawyer."

Mallory nodded, edging to the lip of the dumpster just as Sawyer rolled out, firing his weapon as he jumped up and rushed the alley. She followed suit, laying down cover fire as she ran along the wall, sticking to the deep patches of shadows lined along the edges. Two shots sounded from the far end, then nothing.

Sawyer reached the spot several steps ahead of her, dropping to his knees beside a dark lump. She raced towards them, the body of the girl blurring into view as she got close. Sawyer had one hand on the girl's neck, and the other pressed against her ribcage. Mallory didn't need to look at the wound to know what the bastard had done.

Conflicting emotions warred inside her, and she continued past them, running into the adjoining lane. She slowed just enough to catch a glimpse of the perp flickering in and out of sight halfway down the next alley. He turned just as a flash of light blazed overhead, casting half his face into an almost hallowed glow.

Davies.

Her heart told her she'd only imagined it, but her mind was already three steps ahead. She yelled back to Sawyer and Cole, ignoring their harsh shouts as she took off, sprinting after the creep as he neared another laneway.

A new deluge of rain poured from the sky, obscuring her vision as she followed the road, lungs burning, legs working to keep up the pace. She focused on her stride, making each footfall count as she closed the distance, nothing but catching his ass intruding on her thoughts. She watched as he took a sharp bend, darting down a small path between two buildings off to her left. She hit the opening at a full speed, nearly brushing her shoulder on the brick wall. The distance narrowed to a hundred yards, and she kept running, never taking her eyes off him. She knew he was more than close enough to get a shot off, but between the rain and the shifting shadows, she'd be lucky just to clip him.

The man glanced back at her, taking another hard left. She cursed under her breath and slowed enough to make the turn, taking three steps down the wider street before something hit her hard from the right. Mallory's breath caught as her body twisted sideways, bouncing her off a wall and across the pavement. The force of the blow knocked her gun out of her hand, and she heard the barrel skid along the asphalt, the sound fading into a rumble of thunder. She rolled to a stop, pain pulsing through every inch of her body. Footsteps padded in front of her and she had just enough time to raise her head before a fist pummelled her jaw, knocking her back on her ass.

The impact sparked her reflexes, shaking off some of the shock. She shifted her weight, focusing on the man advancing towards her, recovering just enough to grab his foot as he kicked at her ribcage. His voice echoed through the air as she used his momentum to shove his foot skyward, tossing him onto his back. She took the momentary lapse to push to her feet, wincing at the pain radiating from her face. Blood dripped down her chin, but she didn't stop to wipe it away, as three more men emerged from the shadows, hoods shielding their faces, their hands covered in fingerless gloves.

She scanned the alley, but Davies was gone. Anger flared through the pain as she faced off against the punks standing in front of her. "For the love of God — I'm a federal agent and you jackasses are impeding an arrest. Get the hell out of my way before I take you all in for assaulting an officer."

The man closest laughed, spreading his arms wide as he looked around the small area. "I don't see nobody here but us, bitch. And you ain't looking so good."

He shuffled closer as the other two men helped the creep she'd tossed to the ground gain his feet.

The man smiled at her, his teeth flashing white in the afterglow of the lightning. "Now how about you play nice, and maybe we won't kill you." He licked his lips. "But we will make you scream."

Mallory held up one hand, shaking her index finger at him. "Last chance, asshole. Get out of my way before you all get hurt."

He laughed again and the men moved as one. She stood her ground, stopping the first guy with two jabs and a hard kick to the groin. He fell to the pavement and cupped his crotch as two of the other men grabbed her arms. She twisted and dropped, breaking their hold as she lashed out one leg, sweeping one of the men's legs. He hit the ground hard. Another pair of hands grabbed her jacket and lifted her up, smashing her against the wall. Black dots flickered across her vision as her breath wheezed out in a harsh rasp. She growled and slammed her fists down on his elbows, head-butting him as he dropped his arms, releasing her. She shifted forward just enough to turn and finish him with a roundhouse kick to the head.

More hands pushed her back as a voice shouted in the background, words lost to the beating sound of the rain. She hit the wall again, pain sparking through her shoulder. She blinked back the droplets, then a deafening bang bounced off the walls. The man in front of her pulled away slightly, twisting to look behind him. The other two men stopped, turning towards the rear of the alleyway.

Sawyer stood at the head of the street, gun pointed at them, hair slicked back from the rain. "I said, FBI. Step away from my partner."

The man closest to Mallory glanced at her, drawing a knife from his pocket before lunging towards her. She countered his attack, dodging to the side when another shot echoed down the alley. The guy jerked forward then dropped into a crumpled heap on the ground.

Sawyer took a step closer. "What part of FBI don't you gentlemen understand? And the next bastard to touch the lady gets a bullet in his dick. Now get the hell down on the ground before I decide to shoot you anyway."

Mallory stumbled backwards, bracing her weight on the wall as Sawyer growled out more orders, snapping cuffs on the men still moving. She searched the area again, but knew Davies was long gone. She muttered a hushed curse, knowing there was nothing left to chase but her pride. A beam of light broke the darkness as her Jeep rumbled to a halt at the adjoining road and Cole jumped out, gun drawn, face twisted into a scowl. He looked from her to Sawyer and back again, shaking his head as he knelt beside the guy on the ground, checking his pulse.

He pulled out his cell, calling for paramedics as he met her gaze. The look on his face made her turn away. She closed her eyes, wishing she was anywhere but there, when a hand curled around her arm. She opened her eyes to Sawyer's deadly expression. He didn't say a word, just handed over her weapon before turning around and heading to the mouth of the alley as sirens called in the distance. She let her head fall back against the building, feeling every bruise and cut. Davies' face wavered in the darkness, mocking her. He'd won again. Only this time, she had a bad feeling he'd beaten more than just a brush with death.

* * * *

Mallory sat at the bar, a pack of ice in her left hand, a shot of whisky in her right. She'd already had four rounds, and had no intentions of stopping until she'd drained the rest of the bottle. The stool beside her scraped back, and she shifted her gaze just enough to see Cole slide in next to her, a bottle of beer fisted in one hand. She cursed. She'd already made it clear to both men she wasn't in the mood for company, though they'd ignored her for the most part and had accompanied her to the bar just the same. But that didn't mean she had to like it.

He took a long pull, staring at the label for what felt like forever before finally acknowledging her. "How's your jaw?"

She stared at her own glass, trying to ignore the way her face pulsed to the beat of her heart. That first punch had split her lower lip and bruised her cheek, turning her skin a deep shade of purple. It'd started to swell before the paramedics had left the scene and not even an hour's worth of icing it had been enough to lessen the pain.

She shrugged, finishing the rest of her shot. "Fine."

Cole scoffed, banging his beer down on the table. "Fuck, Mallory! Pulling off a dumbass move is one thing. Brushing off the fact you damn near got your ass kicked, let alone raped, is another."

Mallory glared at him, not willing to back down. "I didn't get my ass kicked, Cole. I was chasing down a suspect when that bastard popped out of nowhere and caught me by surprise. The creep landed a lucky punch, nothing more. And in case you didn't notice, I sent all four of those thugs to the hospital, so don't even start with me."

"Oh, that's right. I forgot. You went all *Jackie Chan* on them, so that makes it okay."

Anger burned through the hurt and she turned, groaning when a sharp pain stabbed through her jaw. "There's another body lying in the morgue bearing all the markings of John Davies." She waved at her face. "So this is getting off easy." She raised the ice pack to her cheek, staring back at her empty drink. "If you only sat down to lecture me, you can find somewhere else to sit. As I already told you, I'm not really in the mood."

Cole cursed beside her, shuffling around as if he couldn't sit still. When she chanced a look his way, he handed her a new pack of ice, taking the old from her and giving it to the bartender. His lips had tensed into a fine line across his face as the muscle in his jaw jumped.

"You are one stubborn SOB, you know that?" He sighed and eased back onto the stool. "So...you sure you saw what you said you saw?"

She snorted, shaking her head. "I'm not sure I was even there at this point. But yeah, it sure as hell looked like Davies. What I saw of him. God knows how that's even possible, but..."

She didn't finish, knowing Cole would draw the same conclusions she had. Either Davies was part of some elaborate, cover-up scheme, or she'd simply seen a ghost.

Or she'd finally lost her mind, which she suspected was Cole's first choice.

She placed the ice against her face, enjoying the numbing coldness. She didn't really care if it was Davies or his ghost, or her mind playing tricks on her, all she wanted was for the pounding in her head to stop. And for that, she needed another shot.

She held up her glass, ignoring the heavy sigh Cole gave her.

"I think you've had enough, Mal."

"It still hurts."

He laid his hand across her arm, cupping, not clenching. "The whisky won't fix that. You should go home. Get some sleep. In fact, take a day off tomorrow."

"Is that an order?"

"Fuck, you don't give an inch, do you?"

"I'm only this stubborn when my partner thinks I'm crazy...or are you speaking on Sawyer's behalf?"

Cole chuckled. "I wouldn't presume to speak for him. Besides, I doubt he'll do anything that doesn't involve yelling." He leaned in closer. "So tell me. How long have you two been sleeping together?"

She shifted just her eyes to focus on him. "I only said that to shut you up."

"No you didn't. You both put up a pretty good front, but there's no doubt that you're doing the nasty. I just wondered if it's recent or since that first night a week ago?"

She raised her eyebrow, hoping it didn't start off a chain reaction of pain. "What makes you so certain?"

He nodded over her shoulder. "The way Sawyer's watching you. He hasn't taken his eyes off you since you basically told us both to fuck off and marched over here."

She gritted her teeth against the pain and took a quick glance over her shoulder. The look in Sawyer's eyes stole her breath. It was nothing short of lethal.

She shrugged, slowly turning back to her drink. "He's just pissed. That doesn't mean I'm having sex with him."

"Mallory. I've seen that look on his face before. He might be pissed, but that's fear in his eyes. You scared the shit out of him tonight, and he wouldn't be that upset if he wasn't invested intimately in your wellbeing." Cole took another pull. "And you're lying to yourself if you think it's just sex."

Mallory sighed. Her head hurt far too much to keep up any pretence with Cole. Besides, she had yet to lie successfully to the man. That was how he knew about the marriage. "I had a nightmare that first night he was going to stay in the spare room and..." She raised one side of her mouth into a grin. "He was kind enough to take my mind off of it."

Cole stayed strangely quiet, nodding his head as he downed the rest of his beer. Then he scraped back his stool and threw some money on the bar. "You sure that's wise?"

She laughed. "Hell, no. But..." She forced herself to swallow past the large lump suddenly lodged in her throat. "Damn. You know I'm still in love with him." She waved it off. "I'll be fine."

Cole patted her on the arm. "Sure. Just know this. If he hurts you again, you'll have to get in line if you want to kill him."

She gave him a smile, holding up her glass to the bartender as Cole walked away. She'd worry about Sawyer later, once she was too numb to care. The bartender shook his head, but filled her glass, giving her a hard look. She nodded her thanks, sliding it across the polished wood until it rested in front of her. The brown liquid gleamed in the overhead lights, mirroring the row of glasses above her in the small circle. She closed her eyes, lifting the shot to her lips. A hand closed around hers, stopping the glass an inch away.

Her eyelids snapped open and she twisted her head. Sawyer stood beside her, one hand palmed on the bar as the other curled around hers. He held her stare, daring her to challenge him as he gently removed the glass and set it on the bar. Then he tossed down thirty bucks, his gaze never leaving hers.

"It's time to go. Grab your coat. We're leaving."

"I didn't finish my drink."

He blocked her from reaching the glass. "Trust me, darling. You're done. We're leaving."

He pulled her off the stool, grabbing her jacket as he headed for the door. She stumbled behind him, caught between trying to keep up and wanting to yank herself free. She waited until they'd cleared the door, stepping into the light rain still blanketing the city, before digging in her heels and pulling her arm away.

Sawyer stopped and turned, the anger on his face more than obvious. "I'm not in the mood to argue with you, Mallory. Now get your ass in the car before I pick you up and carry you there."

Mallory glared at him. *Of all the arrogant...* "Fuck you."

Sawyer growled and moved closer, using his size in an attempt to intimidate her. He stared down at her, close enough to touch her but not moving his hands. "We already tried that, but it hasn't seemed to improve your attitude any. You're as reckless as ever."

"And you're still an arrogant prick who thinks he can waltz into my life after missing in action for two years and tell me what to do." She crossed her arms on her chest, praying she didn't fall on her face as the pain in her head blurred her surroundings. "I've managed to survive all this time without you. I think I can make it another night."

Sawyer's expression changed slightly, something akin to guilt flashing across his face. "So that's what this is about? Of all the times, you're picking now to have it out? Fine. What do you want from me? To have me say I'm sorry? Fine. You've got it. I am sorry, Mallory. Sorry I didn't stick around and pressure you some more when you sat up in your bed and screamed at me to get the hell out of your life!"

His words were laced with pain, but she didn't let it stop her. He wasn't the only one hurting.

She held her ground, not backing down when he stared at her, hair wet across his face, his eyes like two dark pools. "I've told you. I don't remember any of it."

"How fucking convenient for you...*darling.*"

She scowled at the endearment, inching closer. "What's *convenient*, lover, is how over the past week, I've managed to tell you I love you, yet I haven't heard anything remotely resembling those words from you."

A broken sob bubbled free as the truth of the statement hit home. That was what was really killing her. That he hadn't reciprocated her feelings and just the thought of him walking away again was destroying what little sanity she'd salvaged.

Sawyer's eyes bulged wide for a second then narrowed as he watched her through lowered lids. His expression didn't soften as he leaned in, grabbing her shirt on her good side. "The only reason I haven't told you I love you is because you're not ready to hear it. And don't furrow your brow at me like you think I'm crazy, because you know it's true." He shook his head, looking at his feet before meeting her gaze again. "Damn it, Mal, you're so close to the edge, Cole carries a straitjacket around in the back of his truck...just in case." He took a quick breath, blowing it out slowly. "Besides, if you can't tell how much I love you with every touch, every kiss, every bloody smile then that's the real fucking problem here. Now I'll ask you again. Get in the car."

Mallory stared at him, stunned. Was she really riding the line that closely? Cole had made his concerns known on more than one occasion, but she'd never thought he was serious.

The sudden realisation zapped the last of her strength, and she didn't fight when Sawyer curled his fingers around her arm again and led her to her Jeep. She slid boneless into the seat, closing her eyes as he shut her door, opening his moments later. He mumbled something to her, but she didn't reply, too lost in thought to notice. A distant hum prickled her consciousness followed by the steady drone of wheels along the road.

The slap of the wiper blades finally roused her slightly, and she looked out of her window, watching the dark landscape rush past the vehicle in a hazy fog. The odd car beamed a circle of light into the interior, but it only served to add to the distance between them. Sawyer kept his gaze focused on the road, nothing more than the occasional shift of his eyes to signal he was watching her.

His words tumbled over in her head, releasing emotions she hadn't realised she'd buried. It felt as if he'd opened a hole in a dam, and nothing she did could stop the steady flow of water through the break. Even as he turned into the driveway, slamming the vehicle in gear, tears gathered near the surface, threatening to unleash at any moment. She bit her lip, hoping the combined pain would give her just a small measure of control.

Sawyer fidgeted in the seat beside her, apparently confused by the way she just sat there, staring at the house as if it she'd never seen it before. She knew he could see the tears pooled in her eyes, and she suspected the sight made him feel uneasy.

The man sighed, slapping one hand against the steering wheel. "Mallory. Look. I know you're royally pissed at me, but...let's just get you inside and into bed. Then I'll sleep in the spare room, or on the couch. Fuck, I'll sleep out here in the Jeep if you want, but..." His words trailed off, as if he didn't know what else to say to convince her to move.

She tried to will her body out of the car, to stop herself from baring the last of her soul to him, but her head wouldn't listen. Instead, she took a deep breath, unable to stop the words from spilling forth. "Do you know why I became a federal agent?"

There was a moment of silence as Sawyer stared at her, his lips slightly parted, his eyes rounded in shock before he slowly shook his head. "Not exactly. But after everything you confessed that first night, I have a feeling it has something to do with your father."

She chuckled, but the sound was hollow and sad. "I wasn't strong enough to stop him. To help my mother."

"You were a kid. That wasn't your job."

"Maybe not, but I could have tried. I could have done something." She turned to look at him, no longer caring about the tears slowly tracking down her face or the broken feeling radiating from her. "I could have told someone. Gotten her help. But I didn't. I just hid in my room, secretly thankful it wasn't me he used as a punching bag."

Sawyer reached over, resting his fingers across hers. He seemed to sense she was too raw for stronger contact and kept his distance. "It wasn't your fault. Your father was a sick man. And your mother had a choice. She just chose to expose you to him."

"After his death, I promised myself I'd never stand by and watch someone get hurt again. That next time, I'd save them." She sighed. "It took a while to understand what that meant, but being a Fed used to make me believe in that promise. I thought I could handle myself…that I could deal with any situation."

She paused, wishing her mouth would just squeeze shut, but knowing she needed to talk as much as she wanted Sawyer to listen. "That night in the alley. When Davies stabbed me…" She closed her eyes, releasing the small sob tightening her chest. "It was the first time since my father died that I realised I wasn't in control. That despite all the training, the gun, I was still that scared, ten-year-old girl hiding under her bed, praying the monster outside wouldn't find me."

"Davies had the upper hand. There wasn't any way for you to try and save that woman and yourself. You chose to sacrifice yourself. Hell of a choice to have to make."

"But I didn't. She still died and I...I lost you." She took a shaky breath, looking out her window again. "I know you and Cole think I'm reckless, but that's not it. It's a choice. A need to feel that I'm strong enough. I don't expect you guys to understand, I mean, fuck, just look at the two of you. You morons can bend steel with your bare hands. I'm not like that." She blew the breath out. "But I am sorry about tonight. I shouldn't have put the two of you at risk like that. It was selfish of me. And I'll do my best to be a better partner in the future, if Cole doesn't wrap me up in that straitjacket first."

She gripped the handle, wanting to leave before she made more of a fool of herself, when his fingers tightened on hers, holding her in place. She cursed her impetuous tongue, wondering why she'd broken down more times in the last several days than she had in the last twenty years, but realising it was too late to take it back. She'd told him everything, and she could only hope he didn't throw any of it back in her face.

Sawyer's fingers brushed along her jaw, staying clear of the swelling as he gently turned her to face him. His eyes had softened with an emotion she didn't dare interpret. He cupped her chin, using his thumb to wipe away the tears still streaming down her face.

"Do you know why Cole and I were so angry tonight?" He placed a finger over her lips, preventing her from answering. "It wasn't because you took off. Hell, I wouldn't have expected any less of you, but damn...stepping onto that street, seeing you face off against four drugged-out assholes. Darling, it was all I could do not to mow them all down. But what scared me the most was watching you handle yourself. I've never seen you fight like that before, and I think both Cole and I realised you didn't need us anymore. Not for a second. Shit, I only shot that guy because I was afraid you'd kill him with his own damn knife, and I figured he'd at least survive a well-placed bullet wound." Sawyer shook his head. "You don't need to worry about being strong enough, or about proving your father didn't beat you. You just need to realise you're human."

"But..."

The rest of the words wouldn't come as the sobs she'd been holding back resurfaced, breaking through the fragile hold she had and shuddering through her. Sawyer cursed under his breath, leaning over and bodily lifting her into his lap, gathering her in his arms as he whispered soothing words in her ear. She fisted his jacket and buried her face in his shoulder, not sure whether to be happy that he was holding her, or scared shitless that he was witnessing her so vulnerable.

Sawyer pulled her close, smoothing one hand down her hair as he tried to rock her on his lap. "God, Mallory. Darling, please—"

She silenced him with a single finger, shifting in his lap until her head hovered in front of his, their noses touching. She nuzzled him, planting gentle kisses along his jaw before stopping in front of him again. "Make love to me."

Sawyer's brow pulled together in a vee as his gaze fell to her bruised cheek then back to her eyes. "I don't want to hurt you."

She gave him a lopsided smile. "You won't."

"Let's go inside and—"

"Here. Now."

He glanced around the tight space. "In the front seat of the Jeep?"

She leaned in closer, brushing her lips over his, tasting the sweet scent of desire on him. "I don't need pillows or silk sheets. All I need is for you to love me."

He smiled, and the tension that seemed to have plagued him since he'd arrived lifted from his eyes. "Then kiss me."

Chapter Seven

Sawyer closed his eyes as Mallory leaned in, softly taking his lips with hers. She moved slowly, tasting his skin, testing the give of his mouth before finally pressing closer and delving her tongue inside. He didn't rush her, allowing her to set the pace, knowing she needed to gather back some semblance of control. Her body trembled against his, sending his protective instincts into overdrive. He should have followed her sooner, had her back and kicked those fucking bastards in the ass when they'd threatened her. Instead, she'd sat next to him, holding back tears as she'd apologised for not being good enough.

Fuck. He was the one who wasn't good enough. Undeserving of the chances she gave him. Though he'd meant every word about her not being ready, a part of him recognised the real reason he hadn't confessed his undying love—he was stone cold scared. Scared she'd turn him away like she'd done at the hospital. That she'd suddenly realise she could do so much better than him...that Cole was a better man—hell, a better friend—than he could ever hope to be.

Guilt rolled through him as she eased back, dragging her mouth down his neck, biting at the muscle in his shoulder through his shirt. God he loved her. Loved the way she touched, the taste of her mouth. How she smiled when she caught him staring at her or how she never seemed to tire of loving him.

He should tell her. Fear or not, she needed to hear him say the words...now, not when she was ready. He cupped her face, drawing it even with his, fighting the feeling that constricted his throat and burned a hole in his gut. Fuck, she was just too damn beautiful.

She gave him one of those smiles, placing her finger across his lips again. "Don't. You were right. You have shown me. So stop worrying about it, and show me again."

Something inside him snapped, and he moved, planting one hand behind her head as he took her mouth with his. She didn't resist his dominance, opening willingly, allowing him complete control. Her taste soothed some of his tension as he slipped his other hand down, popping open her button and yanking the zipper down. The hiss of metal sounded good...sounded right. He eased his hand into her pants, pushing the denim past her hips.

"Shift just a bit for me, darling."

She complied, shimmying left and right as he shoved the fabric lower, finally ridding herself of the bloody jeans. He inched his hand up, moaning when he encountered only skin.

"Damn, Mal. You go commando at work?"

She chuckled against his ear, working the fly on his jeans. "I like the way the seam rubs over my clit sometimes. I imagine it's your hand or your mouth. I swear I nearly came at my desk today thinking about you poised there between my thighs, licking my cleft, warning me to stay quiet."

He growled, moving one hand up to help her push his pants and briefs down to his knees. "Fuck, girl. You know I'll never be able to work at that desk again without imagining you shouting my name as you cream my tongue." He groaned when she straddled his legs again, brushing her pussy over his aching shaft. "Guess I'll have to settle for you creaming my cock, instead."

Mallory made a second pass, coating his skin with warm, slippery fluid. She was hot and wet, and he wondered if he could convince her to bend over the top of the seat and let him lick every drop of honey from her skin.

She answered his thoughts with a slow pass of her nether lips across his shaft, building his need. He reached down and cupped her ass, loving the hiss of pleasure that escaped her clenched teeth. And as much as he wanted to lift her up and spear his cock inside her, he knew she needed more.

He moved his mouth to her neck, ridding her of her holster and gun before slipping his hands under her shirt and easing it over her head. White lace glowed in the light from the dash, accentuating the perfect symmetry of her breasts. They brushed against his chest, her hard nipples like hot brands against his shirt. He skimmed his hands up her side, cupping each firm mound as he teased her buds through the material. The nubs hardened further, poking against the fabric, drawing raspy moans from deep inside her.

He lowered his head, nipping one taut peak before sucking it into his mouth. Mallory arched her back, begging for more. He huffed and twisted the closure at the back, snapping it open and ripping it off her. He tossed it behind him, completely indifferent to whether she ever found the fucker again. Just another barrier gone as far as he was concerned.

Pale, smooth flesh rubbed against his cheek, and he turned his head just enough to slip one nipple into his mouth. He rolled the tiny bud between his tongue and teeth, drawing on it when she moaned his name. He repeated the action on the other side, tasting the combination of woman and floral soap from this morning. He'd never really been swayed by perfume or oils, but damn if her scent didn't harden his cock, straining it against her flesh.

Another splash of light from a passing car brightened the interior, casting her body into harsh relief. Pale skin, dusky pink nipples and flowing chestnut hair comprised his view, her motions ghostlike in the wedge of light.

Mallory undulated against him, rubbing his shaft back and forth along the length of her slit, before tilting her hips and slipping the tip into her channel. A rush of heat seared his skin, and he squeezed his eyes shut to keep from coming. God, only an inch inside her and he was ready to shoot his load like a fucking teenager.

"Damn, Mal. You're too hot for your own good."

She chuckled, leaning in until her lips brushed his earlobe. "For my good…or yours?"

She lowered her weight, sinking him completely within her silken walls. Pressure built along his shaft, sending ripples of need into his balls. She raised her hips, sliding along the length of his cock until he thought he'd pop free, before she lowered her weight again, plunging him back inside.

He threw his head against the seat rest, knowing if he didn't take his mind off the slow caress of her clenching channel, he'd come before he'd given her any form of release. Mallory didn't seem to share his concern. She nipped at his earlobe, shafting him again, faster, harder than before.

"Fuck, darling. I can't move in this goddamn seat. I'm too close…"

He grunted the last few words as she tilted her hips again, changing the angle of penetration. His cock swelled, tunnelling back and forth as she increased the pace, riding him with the sole intent of making him climax. He cursed every drop of her hips, the firm impalement sealing his fate. He tried to slip his hand between them and touch her clit, but the confined space made the feat impossible.

Sawyer clenched his jaw, holding back the fire swirling in his sac. He was dangerously close to losing it, while she didn't seem to be remotely near the same state. Her sudden intake of breath caught him by surprise. He pried his eyelids open, captivated by the look of sheer pleasure on her face as she tilted her head back, a guttural cry passing her lips. Her channel rippled around him, a fresh wash of cream heating his cock and stealing the last of his resolve. He let go, helpless to stop the rush of pleasure through his shaft as his cock pulsed, giving her every drop of semen he had left.

His breath rasped in his chest as she fell against him, her naked body warm and soft in his arms. He gathered her close, dropping kisses along her forehead, content to simply hold her. The distinct contrast of her smooth skin against his shirt made him smile. Though they were far from boring, she'd never asked him to make love to her in the car before, and knowing she hadn't been able, or hadn't even wanted, to wait until they got inside loosened the tight feeling around his chest.

He inhaled, drinking in the familiar scent of sex coupled with the subtle hint of rain. "I really hope your enthusiasm means I don't have to sleep in the damn Jeep."

She smiled against his shirt, pulling back until their gazes locked. "I guess that depends."

"On what?"

"On whether you have the strength to get us inside, 'cause quite honestly, baby, I don't think I can move."

She laid her head down again, burrowing into the crook of his shoulder. Her weight felt right against him, and he couldn't stop from pulling her closer.

"Not sure you'll feel that way when Cole taps on the window in the morning, especially with your ass hugging the steering wheel."

"I can live with him seeing my ass." She pushed upright again. "I think the question is...can you?"

Sawyer growled. She was pushing him, knowing perfectly well how possessive he got. He held her gaze, adjusting his pants before yanking open the door as he shuffled her in his lap, gaining his feet as he leant forward. Mallory gasped and grabbed the keys and her holster before wrapping her arms around his neck as they stepped into the rain.

"Damn it, Sawyer, I'm naked!"

He shrugged, heading for the door. "Better under the cover of darkness than in the morning."

"I could have gotten dressed first."

"Why, when I'd just strip you down the second we got through the door?" He gave her a wicked smile. "I haven't forgotten how badly I wanted to lick that sweet pussy of yours, so don't think you'll be getting any sleep for a while."

She swatted his shoulder, tensing when a passing car caught them in a spotlight. He just shifted her closer, nodding at the front door. She unlocked it and pushed it open, smiling when he slipped them both through, kicking it shut before heading for her bedroom. He pushed open the door, angling towards the bathroom. She inhaled sharply when he eased her down on the counter, knowing the cold surface would be a stark contrast to what his skin had been only moments before. He held her gaze as he ran the water, cleaning them both before picking her up again and walking to the bed.

Mallory smiled as he placed her in the middle of the bed. She set her gun on the side table then held her hand out to him. The simple gesture clenched his heart, and he reached for her, taking her gently to the bed as his lips claimed hers. She sighed contentedly into his mouth, once again giving him control. His cock nudged her sex and he closed his eyes against the rush of emotion. He was a fool to think he'd ever survive without her, and knew, regardless of his fears, he was home to stay.

She kissed his forehead, the soft whisper of his name feathering over his ear.

He drew back, looking down at her. Her hair fanned out across the sheets, the brown colour gleaming in the sporadic flashes of lightning. The blue in her eyes seemed darker, more like the dawning of night on the horizon.

"God, you're beautiful."

Her lips quirked slightly. "Guess I'm lucky you love the colour purple."

He frowned at the reference to her bruise. He didn't like being reminded of the extent to which he'd failed her. He moved one hand, lightly drawing his fingers along the welt. "Not purple...you. I love you."

Her breathing hitched, tears welling silently behind her eyes. He smiled and dipped down for another kiss, his fear drifting away. This was where he belonged, where he needed to be, and he knew he'd wait forever just to have her say yes one more time.

He planted a chaste kiss on the tip of her nose, praying the tears tracking down her cheeks were from love, not regret. "Now as much as I want to make love to you again, I believe I have a promise to keep."

Her brow furrowed. "What promise?"

He shook his head in feigned annoyance. "Weren't you listening when I told you I was going to lick every drop of cream from your body? You really need to work on your attention skills, darling."

He winked as he moved between her splayed thighs, dropping a kiss on her mound.

She wiggled beneath him, a huff sounding above him. "My attention skills are just... Fuck..."

He hummed against her flesh as he lapped at her clit, her voice fading into a moan. Her fingers found his hair as she scraped them along his scalp, sending shivers down his spine. His name lit the air like a prayer as she tilted her hips, seeking a firmer touch. He obliged, pressing his tongue flat against her skin as he licked her from cleft to clit.

"God, Sawyer. I can't..."

His heart raced with male pride as her body tensed, so close to climaxing her muscles quivered in need. "That's it. Come for me."

Her fingers tightened in his hair, tugging on the ends as she convulsed once, then broke, her back arching off the bed as her orgasm hit. He lapped up her release, growling against her weeping flesh before lunging up her body and hilting himself inside her. His sudden penetration sent her over again, and she screamed his name as she spasmed beneath him, her legs locking behind his ass as he pummelled into her.

She met each thrust, begging him not to stop, scratching his back in her need for more. He gritted his teeth, slamming harder, faster, deeper until she shattered one more time, her whispered words of love fading into nothing as her body went limp beneath him.

The truth in her voice pushed him over and he came, his body jerking against hers. He held himself rigid, shuddering through the last of his release before falling to the mattress beside her, his heavy pants loud in the silent room. Mallory mumbled something incoherent and turned into him, her gentle weight pinning him to the bed. He wrapped his arms around her, wondering if there'd ever be a time he didn't hunger for her...didn't feel incomplete without her in his arms?

He nearly laughed at the thought, well aware of the answer. And despite all the distance between them, he'd never regretted marrying her...even if it'd only lasted a moment.

Sawyer closed his eyes. He'd figure it out later, when his thoughts extended past the next opportunity he'd get to make love to her. Mallory snuffled as she burrowed closer, the gentle press of her head on his chest settling his thoughts. She was safe, and he'd make damn sure she stayed that way.

* * * *

Sawyer leant back in his chair, trying not to stare beneath Mallory's desk at the spot she'd so casually mentioned to him the previous night, though the feat was becoming increasingly more difficult as the day wore on. He'd caught himself mentally counting the hours before he could get her in his arms again and inhale the sweet aroma that tempted his senses as he sat across from her, going through more reports.

He glanced over at her, cursing at the purple welt on her cheek. Though the constant icing the night before had kept the swelling to a minimum, the smear of colour was like a permanent tattoo of the incident in the alleyway, and a constant reminder of their inability to get any closer to the truth.

He sighed and closed his eyes, rubbing the bridge of his nose, trying to pinch the growing headache away. He'd barely slept, and the lack of sleep only served to fuel his restlessness. To top things off, they'd just been notified that the doctor who'd pronounced Davies dead at the execution had been found dead in his car as a result of an apparent suicide. And while the man had sworn his assessment was valid, it seemed a bit too coincidental that his death coincided with an actual sighting of the Davies. Now, with nothing further to grasp at, they were back to looking at grainy videos and going over traffic photos to see if they could get even a glimpse of the man Mallory had chased.

"Here, take this."

Sawyer jumped, nearly knocking the coffee in Cole's hand onto the floor. He chuckled and took the cup. "Thanks."

Cole nodded, though the expression on the man's face said their conversation was far from over. Sawyer had been waiting for him to mention something, suspecting it wasn't every day Cole let himself into Mallory's house only to find her naked with her lover.

At least, Sawyer prayed it was the first time, though the man had come close more than once over the past few days.

Sawyer glanced around. Mallory had disappeared somewhere and most of the other agents were busy at their desks. He nodded at Cole. "If you have something to say to me, just say it. But if you keep glaring at me, Don is going to start thinking we're some kind of threesome."

Cole's mouth pinched slightly before he eased back in his chair, crossing his long legs at the ankles. "Just making sure you heard what I had to say that first night."

"The part where you weren't putting the fear of God in me... Yeah, I heard you."

"You sure? 'Cause the last time I checked, Mallory didn't entertain guests in the nude."

"I think we both know I'm not a guest."

"No, you're her husband, who she hasn't seen in damn near two years." He uncrossed his legs and leant forward, resting his massive hands on his thighs. "The same man who swore to me he wasn't here as a vendetta to hurt her."

Sawyer snorted. "Is that what you think? That I'm getting back at her for what happened in the hospital?"

Cole shrugged. "It'd crossed my mind."

"Great to know you have such a high opinion of me."

"Hey, it's not like I don't think you're a great guy, man, but...Mallory's like a sister to me. I consider it my job to make sure she isn't...unhappy."

A hint of a smile tugged at his mouth. "Did she look unhappy this morning?"

Cole had the grace to blush ever so slightly. "She looked like a woman with more stamina than I gave her credit for."

Sawyer let the smile claim his lips. "Look. I appreciate your concern but...I assure you. I'm not fucking with her."

Cole arched an eyebrow at him.

Sawyer rolled his eyes. "Okay, literally, yes, but not in the hit-and-run sense you're worried about. I have every intention on staying right where you found us this morning."

"With her pinned to the wall?"

"You're an ass."

"And you're a goddamn stallion."

Sawyer sighed. "I love her, Cole. I've already asked my superiors in Albuquerque for a transfer back here. I'm not leaving."

Cole studied his face for a moment then eased back, his expression softening slightly. "Just make sure you don't, because I'd hate to have to kick your ass."

Sawyer smiled at him. "You might be built like a fucking gorilla, but I've got speed."

"Speed won't help you once I catch you."

"Then I suppose I'll just have to avoid that." He nodded down the hall. "Fighting you is one thing, but after last night, I'm not so sure I want to take that on."

Cole turned and smiled as Mallory walked towards them, hips swaying, body moving fluidly across the floor.

She stopped just shy of them, her gaze jumping from one to the other. A set of lines bunched the bridge of her nose as she shifted her feet, clutching a manila folder against her chest. "What?"

Sawyer shrugged. "Nothing. We were just talking."

Her gaze fell on Cole as she furrowed her brow at him. "For fuck's sake, Cole, you weren't threatening Sawyer because you walked in on us this morning, were you?"

Cole reclined back in his chair again. "And if I was?"

Mallory shook her head. "Biggest bloody mistake I ever made, giving you a key."

"Screwing's a nighttime sport. You two would be best to remember that."

"Right. Just like the time I caught you with that hot narc in the back of your truck. What was her name? Lola, Leighla…"

"Fuck off."

"Already did, thanks." She turned to Sawyer. "He's an ass."

Sawyer nodded. "We've already discussed that."

She sighed as she rested her hip on her desk, putting her legs dangerously close to Sawyer. He held back a groan, barely stemming the urge to reach out and caress her calf. The woman was a witch, and he had no doubt the spell she'd cast over him would be his downfall. His gaze fell to her groin and he wondered if she'd gone without panties again. If he'd find her hot and wet if he inched his hand inside her pants. Just the thought punched a jolt of pain through his groin as his cock responded, lengthening against his jeans. Mallory didn't seem to notice how he shifted in the seat, trying to get comfortable. He was rock hard…again. Still.

"Good. Now maybe we can get back to work." She opened the folder in her hand and placed a sheet on the end of her desk. "I think we may have a possible connection to Davies. It's a bit of a stretch, but seeing as we have absolutely jack-all right now…"

Sawyer leant forward, scanning the paper. "Who's Arthur Thomas?"

"Thomas served several months on death row with Davies. Turns out, their cells were side by side."

Cole turned the paper, looking at it as he scrunched his face slightly. "So? The guy's either dead or he's still waiting."

Her lips curled into a knowing smile. "Not this guy. Seems he got pardoned about a month ago. He's been a free man ever since."

Cole raised an eyebrow. "Well. That makes him a bit more interesting, doesn't it? What's the scoop on Mr Thomas?"

She shuffled through some papers, pulling out a handful. "The kid's rap sheet is pretty standard. The guy was in and out of juvie, mostly small-time offences, until he got charged with raping a sixteen-year-old girl. He claimed it was trumped-up statutory charges and that they were in a relationship, but the girl's parents had her pursue legal compensation. He did less than a year on a plea bargain only to get hauled back in when the same girl was murdered four months after his release. Seems the evidence was pretty strong, including DNA samples and witness testimony to seeing him with her on the night she disappeared, but Thomas maintained his innocence."

Cole scanned through the sheets. "I don't know, Mal. This doesn't seem like the kind of case that would get him the death penalty."

"It wasn't. As a matter of fact, the case was thrown out of court on a technicality. Apparently the guy's hotshot lawyer found some kind of illegal procedure and the guy walked."

Cole frowned. "So how does that equate to a stay on death row?"

Mallory pointed to the bottom of another page. "It appears Mr Thomas was in the wrong place at the wrong time. He got arrested on a second murder charge a month later, only this time, they were able to connect him to a string of other deaths. The case relied heavily on blood samples found at the scenes that were used to get a warrant for Thomas' home. Apparently they found newspaper clippings and photos of the dead girls in his house, along with a few personal items. Thomas swore they weren't his…that someone must have broken in and framed him, but it didn't stand up in court and the guy was convicted and sentenced to death."

Cole exhaled a loud breath, scraping his chair forward. "So how is this kid walking the streets of Seattle once again?"

She seemed to shake off her thoughts and handed Cole the sheet. "Several months ago, Thomas' lawyer gets an anonymous phone call. The caller tells the man to check the blood samples but doesn't give any further details. The lawyer decides to get the samples retested out of curiosity and they discover a very subtle incongruity. Seems all of the blood smears found at the scenes had traces of CPDA in them."

Cole snorted as he crossed his arms on his chest. "You do know Sawyer just called me a gorilla, right? I have no fucking clue what CPDA is."

She smiled, giving Sawyer a wink. "It stands for citrate phosphate dextrose adenine. It's a fancy compound they use to help preserve the viability of whole blood for transfusions and the like. It extends the shelf life."

The crease on Cole's forehead deepened. "So?"

"So, if the kid left his blood at the scene because he was the perp, why the hell did it have a preserving agent in it?"

Sawyer cursed. "Someone planted the kid's blood at the crime scenes."

"Oh, it gets better." Mallory shuffled through some more papers. "Turns out, the kid was an occasional blood donor. Liked the extra cash—probably helped fund some of his questionable habits. Anyway, it also happens that he'd donated blood a few days before his arrest. Coincidentally, that same clinic had a break-in the night Thomas was there. Doesn't take a genius to connect the dots here, boys."

Sawyer nodded. "So someone frames Arthur Thomas and basically guarantees the kid a short stay on death row. The question is—why? Some kind of vendetta against the kid? Maybe payback for his first acquittal?"

Cole waved his hand. "But by framing Thomas, they let the real killer go free. Doesn't make much sense if you're playing the part of a vigilante."

Mallory's face sobered. "Maybe the perp's motivation wasn't so pure?"

Cole sat back. "How so?"

"What better way to guarantee your own innocence than to solve the case?"

Sawyer frowned. "So you think whoever's behind this wears a badge? That was a federal case. That would make the bad guy one of us."

She shrugged. "Or maybe it's just someone who has access to the evidence. Either way, someone tampered with it. And it was enough to get Thomas a full pardon."

Cole tapped a finger on his lips. "So how does this tie in to Davies, other than the fact they were side by side for a while?"

"There's a chance Davies told Thomas all about his killings, as in every detail. That could make this kid our copycat. And he had access to Davies."

Cole frowned. "But I thought the kid was framed?"

"Guess there's always a chance Thomas really is some sick pyschopath and his acquittal was just a fluke. He could have gotten released and done this to mess with us." She held up another sheet. "But there's another possibility we might want to consider. I did a search of unsolved murders during the time both Davies and Thomas were incarcerated. Guess what turned up?"

Cole groaned. "I don't think I want to know."

"There are another dozen victims with MO's that seem to be a disturbing mix of the two men, but with just enough differences not to set off any red flags unless you're looking for them." She sighed, running a hand through her hair. "It's all speculation. I mean...if you tear Davies' technique apart, I'm sure it'd match a number of other serial killers."

Sawyer shook his head. "Or maybe, the guy behind those other murders is Davies' partner and Thomas was telling the truth."

Cole shifted in his chair. "These are all great theories, but...it doesn't seem to give us any leads, other than Thomas. And if the guy really was framed, he likely won't be much help."

Mallory shook the folder. "There was another coincidence, though it's even more transparent. I checked through the names of the agents who'd worked Thomas' case. One name did pop up." She released a weary breath. "Derek Carter."

Cole scrambled to his feet, grabbing the sheet out of her hand. "Carter? As in, asshole who worked the Davies case with us Carter? The same guy who cried foul if anyone beat him to the evidence and attempted to 'steal his thunder' as he put it?"

"The very same." She nodded at Don's closed office door. "I wondered why Don hadn't gone into any details about Carter's abrupt change in status. I guess Don was trying to save face for the Bureau. Let's face it. It makes us all look bad when one of our group gets pegged with possible evidence tampering. And it was obviously stressful enough to make Carter quit."

Sawyer motioned to the folder. "So you think Carter is connected?"

Mallory sighed and shifted so she could sink down in her chair. Wisps of hair framed her face as she pushed a weary hand through the thick mass. "I don't know. He had access to the evidence." She snorted. "Along with a dozen other agents and a handful of forensic technicians. Shit. I told you this was a stretch. Maybe I'm just chasing another ghost. Maybe Davies got to me more than I thought and my subconscious turned that guy's face in the alley into the very thing I fear the most. Either way, I don't have the answers." She nodded at Cole. "I don't suppose we could get the coroner to take some more samples for us...just to be sure. I'd like Fisher to rerun some of the blood tests. Ensure nothing in the Davies case was tampered with. Who knows? Maybe this was all an elaborate plan to get Davies pardoned too, only it backfired. After all, if Davies had managed that, he never could have been tried for the same set of murders."

Cole shrugged. "It's not like they need the creep's permission anymore. I'll call over. Get them to send a bunch of samples to the lab. But I can assure you

Fisher isn't going to be pleased you're adding to his workload."

"Fisher can kiss my ass."

Cole chuckled. "Right. I'll tell him to get in line behind lover boy, here."

Cole dodged her slap as he darted over to his desk, giving her a wink before picking up the phone. Sawyer didn't hold back his grin as she turned to face him, a light flush colouring her cheeks.

She glared at him. "What are you smiling at? He insulted you, too."

"I'd be more put out if it wasn't true." He moved in closer, levelling his face even with hers. "And for the record. I'll be the only one kissing any part of your delicious body."

Mallory groaned and shoved him away, leaning back in her chair. "So what's your take on Carter and Thomas?"

Sawyer shrugged. "I agree with Cole. Carter was an insecure little runt, who liked to flaunt his power, but I'm not sure he had the balls to do something this involved. He didn't come across as a risk-taker." He glanced away for a moment. "But I also think it's worth investigating. And there's no harm in having a chat with Mr Thomas. Maybe Davies let something slip during his stay."

Mallory nodded, but her eyes still seemed distant. She looked around the room before settling on his face again. "And if these new samples don't match up? Then what?"

He rubbed her shoulder, trying to keep the contact light. "Darling. We made our decisions based on the evidence on hand. If Carter or someone else tampered with that evidence, it wasn't our fault. Besides, not once did Davies cry foul or contest his guilt. If you were innocent, wouldn't you let a few folks in on the secret?"

"You're right. Why confess when you know you'll be sentenced to death? It doesn't make sense."

She smiled up at him, a hint of the tension leaving her expression when Cole slammed the phone down and marched over, his lips pulled tight, his hands balled into fists at his side. He didn't speak, just stood there, shifting his feet as he grumbled under his breath.

Sawyer cringed inwardly, knowing they were in for more bad news. He gave Mallory a pat on the shoulder as he motioned to Cole. "Just tell us the bad news before you make a hole in the floor."

Cole grunted, shoving his fists into his pockets. "All I have to say is this case is fucked up. Seriously, screwed."

Sawyer scoffed. "So it is bad news."

Cole rolled his eyes as he continued to kick at the floor. "The gist of it is, we won't be getting any more samples."

Mallory frowned, pushing to her feet. "Why not? Did Davies refuse?"

"Funny, Mal. Real funny." Cole clenched his jaw. "Actually, the problem is, the morgue no longer has Davies' body."

Mallory cursed. "What the hell? How did the morgue lose a body?"

"They didn't lose it. They released it."

Sawyer knew his mouth gaped open as he stared at Cole. "Dead or not, John Davies was part of a current, multiple murder investigation. How the hell did the morgue get permission to release the body?"

"I'm not sure. They said they got the proper forms faxed to them shortly after I called that first night to confirm Davies was there. They're faxing a copy over as we speak."

Sawyer snorted, following Cole and Mallory over to the fax machine. "This is insane. Who would release a body when there's an active investigation? No one is that stupid."

"Well, apparently someone is." Cole crossed his arms on his chest as the machine beeped. "Let's face it. It's not like they needed an autopsy to confirm cause of death. The guy was executed. They only brought his body here because there wasn't any next of kin available to collect it from the prison. That being said, there had better be a damn good explanation behind this."

Sawyer glanced at Mallory, knowing this new development was the last thing she needed. Hell, she still hadn't come to terms with the stabbing, or the execution. To think someone had taken the body... He forced in a calming breath. Cole was right. There'd better be a damn good reason behind this.

Cole snatched the papers as they slid out, shuffling through them without doing more than scanning his gaze down the pages. Mallory shouldered up beside him, looking at them over his shoulder when he stopped, his eyes bulging wide.

"No fucking way!" Cole slammed his hand on the top of the machine, nearly knocking it off the desk. "This is bullshit!"

He didn't resist when Mallory eased the sheet from his grasp, holding it so Sawyer could read the words. Sawyer skipped down the page, skimming the information as he searched for the identity of the person who'd signed the release. He'd reached the bottom of the page before the name glared off the paper, the black letters mocking him.

Mallory inhaled roughly beside him, her head tilting to the side before she dropped the page and ran a weary hand down her face. "Son of a bitch."

Cole rounded on them, his eyes narrowed, his hands balled into fists. "That's wrong. You know that's a forgery!"

Her lips quirked as she met his stare. "It looks like your signature, Cole."

"You think I don't know that! But I didn't sign any fucking release form. Hell, Mal, I was here, with you, the entire night. Just when do you think I had the time or the inclination to let that bastard go? Dead or not."

Sawyer cringed as he glanced around. Cole's outburst had received more than a few stares directed their way. He moved forward, but Cole stopped him with a hardened stare.

Cole looked pleadingly at Mallory. "Mallory…"

She sighed and smiled, her eyes soft and reassuring. "Do you seriously think I believe that?" She pointed to the paper lying on the floor. "I gave you a key to my house! I think that means I trust you."

Cole's face scrunched up as he swung his gaze between them. "But I thought—"

"You thought what? That I'd toss years of friendship down the toilet because of one fucking piece of paper?" She snorted. "It'll take more than some random act to make me lose my faith in you. But the paper does leave us with a disturbing thought— whoever's behind this knows enough about the system to manipulate it. And if the bastard can pull this off…"

Sawyer nodded. "Then our perp has more resources than we thought. Which means we need to look at this case from an entirely new perspective. One that's far more personal than we'd like."

Cole's expression eased slightly as he relaxed back against a nearby chair. "So you think this was a ploy to cause dissension in the ranks?"

"Doubt, dissension. They both work. After all, what better way to ruin an investigation than from the inside out. If we're too busy fighting among ourselves, we might miss something." Sawyer tapped his finger on his lips. "Fuck, at this point, I'm only guessing. But I think we should pursue the new information. Let's track down Mr Thomas and see if we can get some updated specs on Carter, just in case. If nothing else, he might be able to shed more light on the Thomas case."

Cole pulled out his cell. "I'll call a friend of mine over at the precinct. See if she can get us an address for Thomas. But it might be best to head for the prison. Maybe Thomas had some visitors we can link back to Davies."

"Sounds like a place to start." Sawyer watched Cole walk off before turning to Mallory. "You okay?"

She shrugged. "I don't like being played with. It's like trying to follow someone in the fog."

He moved closer, glancing around before giving her shoulders a quick squeeze. "That's not what's really bothering you, is it?"

She sighed. "Have I ever told you that you're a real pain in the ass?"

"Multiple times."

Mallory groaned and looked skyward as if searching for some form of intervention. But her smile faded as she met his gaze. "Doesn't it bother you just a bit that not only does the doctor, who pronounced Davies dead, apparently kill himself just days after the execution, but Davies' body goes missing after only a few hours in the morgue?"

"You mean, do I believe that somehow the bastard is still alive?"

Her mouth turned down in defeat. "Do you?"

"It's doubtful. Do you have any idea the lengths someone would have to go to just to fool everyone, never mind the access and resources they'd need to pull something like that off? I mean, there's the prison, the medical staff, us... It's a tall order to fill. It'd take more than one man to make that happen."

"But not impossible."

He released a slow breath. "No. Not impossible."

"Fuck."

Sawyer grabbed her hand, not caring if anyone saw. "If he is somehow still alive, I won't let that monster hurt you again. Period."

She smiled, patting his cheek before pulling away. "It's not me I'm afraid for."

Sawyer cursed as she moved past him, her shoulders slightly hunched. Damn Davies. The bastard had already broken them up once. There was no chance in hell that Sawyer was going to let the creep hurt them again.

He followed her back to her desk, watching as she shuffled papers around the top. He could tell by the way she slammed stuff down a bit too hard that she wasn't happy with the new twist, but shit, neither was he. She was right. They were being played and by someone who had intimate knowledge of the system.

Cole marched up beside him, his face a grim mirror of Mallory's. "My friend's trying to find a current address for Thomas. Until then, let's head over to the prison. If nothing else, we might get a handle on who visited the guy and if there's any kind of connection we didn't see before." He held up his keys. "I'll drive."

Mallory shook her head as she grabbed her jacket off the back of her chair, giving Sawyer a fleeting smile. "Fine, but we're stopping for coffee on the way. Hell, make it whisky."

"Coffee. And lover boy's buying."

Cole winked at Sawyer as he darted away, a deep chuckle drifting across the space. Sawyer smiled and motioned Mallory ahead. At least Cole seemed more relaxed, which was more than he could say about Mallory. And he had a bad feeling the tension was just beginning.

Chapter Eight

Sawyer sat in the car, listening to the steady drone of the tyres along the pavement as Cole wove his way through a tangle of residential streets. They'd grabbed a coffee, but the incessant ringing of Cole's phone had meant a change of course. Sawyer had asked the man where they were headed, but Cole had simply mumbled something about *them seeing when they got there* and had left it at that. Now Sawyer was forced to stare out the window, watching the cookie-cutter houses pass as a brown blur outside the truck. Even the hint of sunshine wasn't enough to brighten his mood.

He glanced in the rearview mirror at Mallory, but she'd fallen asleep with her forehead resting on the glass, her long lashes dark against her pale skin. He frowned. He wasn't sure how much more she could take. Though she put up a good façade, he knew it was only a matter of time before the walls crumbled, and she'd be forced to face the full impact John Davies' actions had inflicted on her. God help them if Davies turned up alive.

He shook the thought away. It was a pipe dream at best. Faking one's death was the stuff of Hollywood, and Davies was a B-movie actor at best. More than likely the real creep behind the deaths was using Davies as a means to get to them—to Mallory. Unfortunately, it was working.

He sighed, making a mental note to talk to her later, only this time he wouldn't let his dick lead the conversation. She needed to come to terms with the stabbing, with their renewed relationship. Hell, he needed her to know he was in this for the long run—and not just to share her bed. He wanted to share her life.

The squeal of brakes shook him from his thoughts and he turned towards Cole as the man shoved the truck into park. Sawyer glanced at the area. More of the same houses lined the street, with the exception of a school at the end of the block. Nothing seemed out of the ordinary and he couldn't help but wonder why Cole had stopped here.

Sawyer cracked open the door, stepping onto the kerb when the back door lurched open and Mallory all but fell out of the truck. She looked dazed, her gaze focused on the bungalow across the street. He glanced over at it, noting the chipped paint and overgrown yard. Either the place was deserted or the owner simply didn't give a shit.

"Mallory?"

She ignored him, rounding the truck before stumbling to a halt. He glanced at Cole, but the man shrugged, calling her name. She didn't respond to Cole either, bracing some of her weight on the tailgate as she continued to stare at the home as if she saw something neither of them did.

Fear tugged at the edge of his consciousness, quickening his heart rate slightly. He moved over to her, snagging her arm as she started to cross the street. She resisted for a moment, pulling against his hold before turning to look at him, her mouth a thin line across her face.

He narrowed his eyes, more than aware of the fear reflected in hers. "Mallory?"

Her brow furrowed as she shifted her gaze between the two men. She yanked her arm free, stumbling backwards a step before glaring at Cole. "What the hell is this? Some kind of joke? Because I assure you, it isn't funny."

Cole looked at Sawyer, confusion clearly etched on his face, as he faced Mallory. "Are you okay? And what do you mean by joke?"

Mallory continued to glare as she pointed at the house behind her. "That! Why the hell are we standing here, staring at that? I thought we were going to the prison or hunting down Thomas?"

Cole held his hands up, obviously trying to soothe her. "Mal. I don't have a clue what you're talking about. We are hunting down Thomas." He motioned to the house. "This is his last known address."

The colour drained from her face as her mouth hinged open in apparent shock. She glanced behind her, almost as if she wasn't certain what she'd find, before shaking her head, her hands trembling as she raised them beside her. "That is Thomas' residence?" She shook her head. "There's got to be a mistake. He can't live there. What kind of bullshit is this?"

She reeled backward and Sawyer grabbed her as a car sped past, barely missing her. He pulled her tight to his chest, his heart racing, his breath coming in strangled pants. He didn't know what the hell she was talking about, but he knew her intimately enough to tell she was terrified.

He held firm as she struggled against him, her back rigid, her hands pressed hard on his ribs, until her body finally relaxed, her head turning to rest on his chest. He didn't speak as a hushed sob broke free, the simple sound making his heart squeeze tight. She took a ragged breath then eased away, wiping at the wash of tears staining her cheeks.

Sawyer held his ground, not letting her get more than a foot away. "Better?"

She nodded, though he could tell it was more for his benefit than because she actually felt any form of relief. Cole moved in beside them, his forehead creased as he stared at her. She offered an apologetic smile, but it didn't reach her eyes.

Sawyer gently clasped her hand, holding it in his as he motioned to the house. "Think you can tell us what's going on? What has you so freaked out?"

Her chin quivered for a moment before she visibly drew herself up, her throat bobbing as she swallowed forcefully. "It's Thomas' house, or should I say, my house."

Sawyer glanced at Cole, but the man didn't seem any the wiser, darting his gaze between them and the bungalow across the street. If he knew anything, he'd hidden it well.

Sawyer pursed his lips, knowing he had to tread carefully. "Your house? I wasn't aware you owned another home."

Her mouth turned down at the edges as she exhaled, looking as if she wanted to hit him. "It's not mine anymore." She turned her head away, adding, "Sometimes I wish it never had been," under her breath.

Understanding dawned on him and he stared at the house again. Though it looked unassuming, he had no trouble imagining the horrors she'd describing playing behind the closed curtains and shrouded walls. He clenched his jaw, not sure what to say when Cole muscled in.

"Don't take this the wrong way, Mal, but..." He closed the distance, pointing to the bruise on her cheek. "Are you sure you didn't get a concussion last night? 'Cause the last time I checked, I had a key to your house, and this ain't it."

She spun around to glare at him again. "Seriously, Cole? You just missed the whole part where I said it wasn't mine anymore?" She huffed out an irritated breath. "This was my childhood home. You know...the place where my mother decided to redecorate my room with my father's blood!" She gazed at the place over her shoulder. "I haven't been back since the police dragged me out of there."

Cole cursed and slammed his hand down on the back of his truck. He looked ready to strangle someone. "Fuck. Are you sure?" He groaned and waved the question off. "Of course you're sure. It's not something you'd forget. But I mean... Shit. What are the chances the guy we're trying to link to Davies just happens to live in the same house where your mother killed your father?"

She clenched her jaw. "I'd say about zero." She shook her head. "Come on. Even I realise this isn't some weird coincidence. First, the killer starts marking his new victims with the same wound Davies gave me. Then he picks the alley where I got stabbed. Now the trail has led us back to my version of the Amityville Horror house. You can't tell me this wasn't planned. Sawyer's right. This is personal...intimate."

Sawyer grimaced. "I was actually hoping to be wrong in this instance." He nodded at Mallory. "And when the hell did you tell Cole about your parents?"

Mallory scoffed. "I don't think this is the time or the place to get pissy over that."

"Isn't it?"

She glared at him.

"Fine." Sawyer pushed down his sense of disappointment. While he didn't care that Cole knew about her past, he'd be lying if he didn't admit it hurt.

Mallory cursed and stomped a foot on the ground, a deep flush colouring her cheeks. "Look, if I'd had my way, neither of you would know, but Cole had the misfortune of being at the house when the damn prison called to inform me my mother was refusing medical care. It's not the kind of call you can lie your way out of, especially when you need a ride to the bloody facility to sign a bunch of forms to legally enforce the treatment. Now can we please get back to why the hell Thomas is living in my old house?"

"You need a better reason than to mess with your head?" Sawyer motioned at the three of them. "We were mostly responsible for Davies' capture, and his ultimate sentence. So whether this is Davies reincarnated or some deranged partner, I think it's safe to say they're just trying to get to us." He nodded at her. "To you. Let's face it, Mallory. Stabbing a Fed was Davies' biggest mistake. The DA might have gone for multiple life sentences if he hadn't nearly killed one of their own. Everyone knows there's no coming back from that. As soon as he stuck that knife in your side, he was a walking dead man."

"How apropos since he still seems to be one." She sighed and glanced at the house again. "So now what?"

Cole shrugged. "We stick to the plan and go have a chat with Mr Thomas." He inched closer. "I'd suggest you stay in the truck, but then you'd probably hit me."

Mallory chuckled, patting Cole on the shoulder. "And to think you didn't want to take over as my partner."

"Just my luck no one else would have you."

"Then I guess that means you're stuck with me...here, too."

Cole sighed, but nodded, checking the street before shambling across. Mallory took a deep breath and turned to follow, when Sawyer snagged her wrist. She stumbled to a halt, glancing at his hand before meeting his gaze, her question clearly stated by the arch of one eyebrow.

Sawyer held his ground. "Cole might not want to face your wrath, but I'm more than up for the job. So answer me one thing before we go inside."

She schooled her features. "All right."

"Tell me there's no chance of you freezing up in there, and I'll gladly have you watch my back. But if you think, even for a moment, that place might be too much..."

He didn't finish, more than aware he'd made his case. Mallory's mouth pulled tight as she shifted on her feet, her gaze darting between the truck and some spot on the pavement. Another car passed behind them before she released a weary breath and raised her face to his.

"I'll be okay." She raised her hand, silencing any further questions. "I'm not about to put your life or Cole's at risk. But I can handle this. We might be chasing a ghost, but it's not my father's, so it's good."

Sawyer stared at her eyes, watching fear wash in and out of them. While he had no doubt she was scared, he could read the honesty in her expression.

He offered her a reassuring smile. "Just do me a favour and try not to go all *Jackie Chan,* as Cole puts it, on anyone before we question them."

She swatted his shoulder. "I'll do my best."

Sawyer simply nodded and followed her across the street, meeting up with Cole on the porch. He didn't speak, just stood there, scanning the area, as Sawyer approached the door. The room beyond the windows looked dark and Sawyer had a bad feeling this wasn't going to go as they'd hoped.

He rang the doorbell, stepping back as he kept his attention on the door. After a minute, he banged his hand on the wood, secretly praying someone would open up.

"There's no one here." Mallory moved forward, twisting the knob. It gave easily in her grip, the edge of the door sliding open. She glanced at the wedge of space then at Sawyer. "And I'm supposed to believe the man doesn't lock his door, whether he's home or not?"

Cole snorted. "Maybe he just has faith in his fellow man."

Mallory all but rolled her eyes. "Right. A wrongly convicted felon who's just spent a year on death row has faith in his fellow man. That seems reasonable." She looked at Sawyer. "I'd say our reason for knocking on his door is just cause for taking a peek inside, don't you?"

Sawyer grinned. "I don't know about the two of you, but I'm genuinely concerned for Mr Thomas' welfare. It wouldn't be right not to ensure he's not trapped under heavy furniture and unable to get to the door."

"Exactly." Mallory nodded at Cole. "You want to go first?"

"I'll go around back. Make sure our friend isn't hopping the fence."

The edges of Mallory's lips turned down slightly. "You sure that's wise? Might be better not to split up."

Cole flashed her a beaming smile. "It's standard protocol to have one agent secure any alternate entryways. Besides, I thought you said I was the brawn in our relationship."

"Just don't shoot Thomas if he is trying to run. We need answers."

"Then I'll be sure not to shoot him in the mouth." He winked at her, jumping off the porch as he headed for the rear yard.

Mallory sighed. "That man is insane."

"Of course he is. He took you as a partner, didn't he?"

Sawyer dodged her slap and eased the door open, palming the grip of his gun as the old hinges creaked in protest. A triangle of light spread out across the floor, casting the corners of the room into shadows. A scattering of furniture filled the living space, making the room feel desolate. Deserted.

"Mr Thomas? FBI. We'd like to ask you some questions."

An eerie silence filled the house, prickling the hairs on the nape of his neck. There was something unnatural about the way the house was arranged. It felt more than on display and Sawyer had a bad feeling they were walking into a trap.

He drew his gun, blocking Mallory's way when she went to step by him. He didn't speak, just gave her a hardened stare. She clenched her jaw, but nodded, following his lead as he moved inside, slowly closing the door behind them.

He leaned in close. "We'll go together. Clear one room at a time."

"I should lead." She held up a finger when he opened his mouth to protest. "I used to live here. I think that means I'm familiar with the layout."

He cursed but nodded. If it were any other location, he wouldn't second-guess her taking lead. He needed to show her he trusted her. "I've got your back."

A wicked smile spread across her face before she turned, heading for the door on their right. She stayed quiet, using hand signals to announce her intentions. As she mouthed three, she threw open the door, her gun sweeping the space as he covered her from behind. Nothing moved in the small office as she checked behind the door before moving forward again.

They cleared the kitchen next, checking the pantry and closets as they went. Sawyer tried not to imagine an older version of Mallory lying in a pool of blood on the floor, but Mallory's words from that first night made the image waver in his head. God, how many times had that story played out? How had Mallory not succumbed to a much darker personality?

He watched her move. If being in the home made her uneasy, she wasn't showing it, not that he expected her to. She was nothing if not stubborn and after stating she'd be fine, he knew she'd rather suffer in a silent hell than show him or Cole any trace of anxiety.

He sighed, finally grabbing her arm as they made their way back to the hallway. She glanced at him, confusion in her eyes as she motioned up the hallway.

He tried to smile, but knew it was probably more of a grimace than anything. "Are you sure you're okay being in here?"

The lines around her mouth creased ever so slightly as she drew herself up. "I told you I would be."

He sighed and brushed a finger along her jaw before dropping it to his side. "I know what you said, and I'm confident you won't let so much as a glimmer of disgust cross your face but... Shit. This place. It's..."

She scoffed. "Wrong. Yeah, I know. I grew up here, and I can assure you it was just as creepy and evil back then." She punched his arm. "I'm not going to lie and say I'm having a good time, but...I'm okay. I know my dad can't hurt me so it's not quite as bad as I feared it'd be."

"Good. Because I swear I'm one second away from running out the door." He gave her a genuine smile this time. "Let's keep going, before Cole breaks down the back door."

She lifted the corner of her lips slightly and moved down the hall, walking with a familiarity that still unnerved him. And here she thought she wasn't strong enough. If only she realised how wrong she was.

They cleared what looked like the master bedroom then came to the last door on the left. She stopped and he couldn't help but notice it was the first time she'd hesitated.

He moved closer, nudging her. "Something wrong?"

She shrugged and reached for the handle. "This was my room."

She didn't elaborate, but she didn't need to. He suspected what was going through her mind. How the room had looked the last time she'd been there and how those images must still linger.

He rested his hand on hers, motioning for her to step back. She looked as if she was going to argue, then silently relented, moving behind him as he palmed the handle. The knob creaked as he turned it, and he readied his gun before swinging it open. Light beamed through the open window, making the room oddly bright compared to the rest of the house. He blinked against the sudden glare and took a step forward, then stopped dead.

"Holy shit." He covered his mouth with the back of his hand, trying not to taste the metallic scent hanging in the air. "Mallory, don't—"

Her gasp cut him off, and he turned. Her face looked whiter than he'd ever seen it, as her gaze travelled the room, from the blood arced across the ceiling and quilt, to the teenage girl mutilated and posed on the bed, before settling on the man lying face down on the floor, more blood pooled around his chest as it dripped from several puncture wounds along his back. Something akin to a whimper passed her lips before she backed up, bending over and resting her weight against the wall.

Sawyer moved in front of her, keeping her at his back as he kept watch at the door. This wasn't a random killing, and while he hadn't tracked down the crime photos from Mallory's family, he had a pretty good guess that this was a close approximation of what her bedroom had looked like after the murder, though the fact the killer had included another victim in place of Mallory was more than disconcerting.

Mallory grabbed his shoulder. "I don't need protecting."

"Do you honestly think the bastard who did this didn't stick around to see your reaction? While there are a shit ton of questions I have no answers for, the one thing I'm certain of is...we aren't alone."

"Fuck. Cole's still outside. Alone."

"We'll get to him. Just stay close and don't even think of darting off after anyone. Got me?"

She met his gaze, a flash of hurt in hers. "Weren't you listening last night when I told you I wanted to be a better partner—in every sense of the word? Now stop treating me like a child and let's get Cole."

He didn't stop her as she pushed past him, clearing the hallway before darting down it. She'd mentioned there was a small mudroom at the end of the house, and he assumed she was headed there. He followed after her, listening for any hint of movement as they stopped at the back door. It didn't look as if Cole had made it to the rear porch yet, and that thought sent a cold shiver down Sawyer's spine. The man should have been inside the house by now.

Mallory peeked out a window. "Cole should be here. Where the hell is he?"

"Maybe he couldn't gain access to the yard?"

She scoffed at him. "I've seen him scale fences bigger than the one lining this house. No way something like that stopped him. And if it did, then why didn't he just follow us in the front?" Her mouth quirked. "I don't like this."

"Cole can handle himself. But if he is hurt, getting ourselves killed won't be the rescue he needs."

"So help me, if Davies has so much as touched him..."

Her words faded as shouts erupted outside, followed by a shot. Sawyer didn't wait to find out who they belonged to. He grabbed the handle and yanked the door open, barrelling through as he cleared each side then jumped onto the ground, searching for any sign of Cole. Another shot rang out and he grabbed Mallory as she moved in beside him and pulled them both behind a planter.

Mallory cursed, popping up to get a look before ducking back down. "I think it's coming in the direction of the shed, but I'm not sure. I didn't see shit."

"Me, either." Sawyer checked the yard. "I'll go on three. You cover me and when I reach the shed, I'll cover you."

"I'm faster."

"Like hell you are." He nodded at her. "On three."

He mouthed the numbers, cleared the area then bolted, running for the shed at the rear of the yard. He saw Mallory dart out, scanning the area, but she didn't fire, following on his heels once he'd reached the outbuilding. She rolled in behind him, brushing off the dirt as she pushed to her feet next to him. She looked as worried as he felt, and he knew if Cole had been killed, it'd be the final straw that pushed her over the edge.

He scoured the landscape, catching a hint of movement over behind a group of fruit trees. He pointed to the copse. "Someone's over there."

Mallory peered at the spot, her breath stalling. "Damn, it's Cole."

"How can you tell?"

"He always wears that stupid leather jacket. I'd know it anywhere."

She moved to dart out when Sawyer snagged her wrist.

"It could be a trap. Someone else wearing Cole's jacket to lure us there."

She looked over at him. "Then I'll blow their brains out once I get there."

He grimaced, knowing nothing short of shooting her would stop her from going to Cole's aid, whether he needed it or not. "Fine. You start off. I'll cover you in case that is Cole and we still have a gunman on the loose."

She nodded, took a deep breath then ran, covering the distance at a full sprint. She dove to the ground as she neared the trees then disappeared behind them. Sawyer searched the fence line, but nothing glared out at him. He cursed and took off running, praying he hadn't allowed Mallory to walk into a setup as he raced across the yard, finally ducking in behind the trees. Cole had his back to one of the trunks, a line of blood dripping down his arm. Mallory had managed to get his jacket off and was busy accessing a blackened wound on his shoulder. Another body slouched against the tree next to Cole, but Sawyer could tell the woman was dead, her blank eyes staring at nothing.

Mallory knelt beside him, wadding up a piece of her shirt on the wound. She didn't speak, just held it tight as she kept watch around them.

Sawyer went to his knees. "Guess you drew the short straw this time."

Cole scowled, grunting as Mallory increased the pressure. "That damn gate was harder than shit to get open. Then I saw the woman as I came around the side, but when I tried to see if I could revive her, our perp popped out from behind the shed. I yelled at him to stop, but he landed a lucky shot." He winced as Mallory added another wad, layering it on top. "I fired one back, but he'd disappeared."

Sawyer nodded, tilting his head as sirens blared in the distance. Seemed Cole had already called for backup. "You get a good look at the guy?"

Cole's eyes creased at the edges as a line formed across the bridge of his nose. He glanced at Mallory then sighed. "It looked like Davies — same hair, same angular nose and beady little eyes — but, shit, I can't swear on it."

"I'll take your word." Sawyer patted Cole on the leg. "Rest. Even a brute like you might run out of blood."

Cole scoffed at him. "Not likely. It barely made a scratch."

Mallory snorted and shook her head. "It went clean through your shoulder muscle, you big jerk. So I'd call it more than a scratch." Mallory motioned to the dead woman beside them. "Our killer left another one inside, along with a guy. I'm betting the corpse is Thomas."

Cole's eyes widened and he glanced at Sawyer before looking back at Mallory. "Where did you find them?"

Mallory forced down a swallow then turned away.

Cole swore, slamming his good hand on the ground. "Fuck. The bastard did something inside, didn't he? What did he do?"

Mallory grunted and grabbed Sawyer's hand, placing it on the wound. "Keep the pressure on. I'll go make sure the paramedics don't miss the house. They sound like they're just down the street."

She bolted before either of them could get a word in, her back stiff as she made for the gate, constantly checking behind her, finally rounding the side of the building. Sawyer growled under his breath, trying to stem the anger welling inside him. Whoever was responsible would pay...one way or another.

Cole reached for Sawyer's hand, drawing his attention. "What the hell did the bastard do inside, Sawyer?"

Sawyer released a slow breath. God, he was tired. Tired and angry and just too damn close to see anything but the pain on Mallory's face. He met Cole's gaze. "He turned Mallory's old bedroom into a murder scene...one that I think hit a bit too close to home. My guess is the creep recreated her father's death, only with a new twist. He left a dead woman on the bed."

"Goddamn, son of a bitch! I knew it. I knew there was something wrong with this case the moment Fisher called us in the middle of the damn execution. I told Mal nothing good was going to come of this, and well, fuck!"

Sawyer nodded, not sure what else to say. They were constantly a step behind and if they didn't catch a break soon, Davies might not be the only ghost they ended up chasing.

Chapter Nine

Sawyer leaned against the doorframe, watching Mallory as she sat at the living room bar, her head bowed, staring aimlessly at the top of the table. A glass of whisky loomed dangerously close, though she hadn't done more than glance at it. They'd spent several hours at the hospital, waiting while the doctors had treated Cole. Twenty stitches and a couple of pints of blood later, the man had been taken to a room, much to Cole's annoyance. They'd cited something about watching him for twenty-four hours, but Sawyer knew just being in that environment had taken a toll on Mallory.

He ambled in, taking a seat next to her. He didn't talk, just sat there, his arm touching hers as she thumbed at a coaster tossed on the counter. Silence stretched out between them until she finally sighed and rested her head on his shoulder. The gentle weight triggered something inside him. She'd never allowed him to be strong for her before, and the simple act made his heart soar.

He ran a hand down her hair, loving the feel of the silky strands across his skin. "Are you sure you don't want that whisky?"

She snorted and lifted her head, gazing at him. "Whatever happened to asking me if I was okay first?"

He shrugged. "I already know you're not. I'm just trying to gauge how far from okay you've slipped."

Her eyes softened and she gave him a hint of a smile. "Before you came back, about half a bottle's worth. But now?" She leaned into his shoulder again. "This seems about right."

A fluttering feeling lighted in his heart, and he wrapped one arm around her shoulders, pulling her closer. Her breath feathered over his neck, the subtle breeze soothing the rawness he'd felt inside since opening the door to her old bedroom. After that experience, he'd half expected to find her rocking in the corner of their bedroom, mumbling Davies' name over and over, and the simple statement that his presence was all she needed to stay sane more than humbled him.

He closed his eyes against the sudden sting of tears, not sure where all this emotion had come from. He wasn't one to fall for sappy movies, or endearing sentiments, but something about the ease with which she gave herself over to him, trusting he'd keep her safe, hit home.

He smiled, holding her tight as he dropped a kiss on her hair. "Does that mean I get the whisky?"

She chuckled. "Maybe I can offer you something better?"

"That sounds promising." He paused, not wanting to break the sensuous atmosphere but aware they still needed to talk about what had happened. Silence was what had got between them before, and he wouldn't make the same mistake twice.

He took a deep breath. "Now before you rob me of every coherent thought, I think we should talk about what happened."

Her body stiffened against his, her breath an audible rasp through her teeth. She pulled back, giving him a hardened look before standing and making her way over to the fireplace. She set her jaw, finally glancing over at him. "I think we've talked enough."

"Funny, I was thinking the exact opposite." He held up his hand as he pressed to his feet, covering the distance between them. "I realise talking about your past isn't high on your list of pleasurable pastimes, but damn, until a week ago, I had no idea about your parents and after that hadn't even considered that the fucking house was still standing." He paused, gathering enough strength to finish his reasoning. "I lost you once because I didn't have the courage to ask the difficult questions. I have no intention of repeating that."

Tears misted her eyes as she turned away, a shudder trembling through her. He waited, knowing the choice had to be hers. The clock on the mantel ticked loudly in the quiet until she cursed and moved into his arms, resting her head in the crook of his shoulder as he folded his arms around her. She didn't cry, just stood there, breathing heavily as her fingers clenched his shirt. He dropped kisses on the top of her head, silently willing her to break the tension, when she eased back, wiping a stray tear from her cheek.

She toed at the floor, darting her gaze between her foot and his chin. "Fine, though I don't know what my past has to do with any of this, other than the obvious."

"It's like you said. This isn't a coincidence. Someone is going to some pretty extreme lengths to push you off the sanity deep end, and I have a bad feeling it's rooted in that night."

She finally met his stare. "I already told you what happened. There isn't anything else worth mentioning."

He tried to soften his expression as he took her hands in his. "What happened after your mother killed your father? Did she try to run?"

Mallory snorted. "My mother? Run? The woman had spent over a decade playing housemaid to a man whose only redeeming quality was not killing her outright. She didn't leave the house. Just walked into the living room and sat down on the couch, blood splattered across her clothes, the knife still dangling from her fingers. That's how the cops found her."

"Where were you during that time?"

Something passed through her eyes, though he couldn't tell if it was regret or terror.

She coughed as she tried to swallow, before staring at the floor again. "During the incident, he fell on top of me on the bed. He weighed so much more than me, I couldn't—"

"She left you there! With that fucking bastard dead on top of you?"

Mallory winced at the hatred in his voice, nodding solemnly as she continued to kick at the floor. "I called for her for I don't know how long, but I guess she'd given me all she could. I'd managed to roll him off of me and move over to the corner of the room when the cops showed up. They said a neighbour heard me screaming, heard my father raging, and called them." Her gaze turned slightly vacant, as if she was remembering the scene in her mind. "I didn't see her again until I had to testify in court. I wanted to, but...the lawyers thought visiting would damage my credibility."

"Credibility? Against your own mother?" Sawyer closed his eyes against the rush of anger. God, the story just kept getting worse. He forced his eyelids open and cupped her chin, waiting for her to look him in the eyes. "I can't believe they made a ten-year-old testify in court."

Somehow, she held his gaze without wincing. "Her appointed lawyer hoped it would get her sent to a psychiatric facility instead of the penitentiary. The guy claimed she had some kind of personality disorder, but it didn't hold up in court."

"Dear God." He shook his head, wanting nothing more than to hold her and never let go. But there had to be something about the murder that was linked to the new killings. He brushed his finger along her jaw before letting his hand drop back to his side. "What about since then? Have you ever discussed what happened with your mother?"

Her face paled. "She hasn't spoken a word to me since."

Fuck. "Nothing?"

Mallory tilted her head in a way that told him everything. "I used to visit her every week. The rare times she'd actually bother to come to the window, she just sat there, staring through me. Over the years, I went less and less until I just stopped. What was the point? She couldn't even look at me."

Sawyer raised his hands, wrapping them gently around her shoulders. "None of this was your fault. You know that, right?"

"Wasn't it?" She backed away, motioning for him to listen. "She never wanted kids. Never wanted to be

155

tied to my father more than she already was. When I came along, I was just something else he could use to hurt her. When I didn't put my toys away properly, or clean my room just right, it was another excuse for him to hit her. I grew up having my mother pay the price for me being born, for not being perfect. So yeah. I didn't murder the bastard, but you can't stand there and tell me I wasn't the cause." She lowered her head and took a shaky breath. "I know in my head that they were sick, that I was just collateral damage, but..." She met his gaze again. "It doesn't stop the nightmares from coming or from me feeling as if I'm fighting his ghost at every turn."

He waited for her to steady her breathing before giving her an encouraging smile. "After the way you handled yourself today, I'd say you've vanquished that spirit." He moved in front of her and held out his hand. "Come on. What do you say to a warm shower and my shoulder as a pillow for the night?"

Her lips quirked into the beginnings of a smile before the bottom one trembled slightly. "You won't let go?"

He smiled past the clenching of his heart at the broken quality to her voice. "You promise not to snore?"

The smile resurfaced. "I never snore. You, on the other hand..."

He shook his head. "Then it's a promise."

She took his hand, slipping in beside him and following him down the hall and through the bedroom door, tugging on his hand as he headed for the bathroom. Her eyes looked wider than normal as she glanced around the room before settling on his face. She released a long breath, as if she'd been holding it in anticipation. "I don't want you to leave."

Confusion raised one eyebrow as he gave her what he knew was a half-smile. "I'm pretty sure I just promised to hold you all night."

"Not that. I mean after."

"After?"

"When the case is over. I don't want you to go back to Albuquerque. In fact, I don't want to leave the house."

Sawyer sighed and tugged her into his arms. "I don't want to leave the house, either." He inhaled, savouring the scent of warm woman and floral soap. "I was waiting for the right time to tell you, but I requested a transfer back here."

She pulled away, raising her face to his. "You requested a transfer? Back here? When?"

He couldn't contain his smile. "A couple of days ago. I wanted to know it was a viable option before mentioning it."

"No. You wanted to make sure I wasn't going to freak out before mentioning it."

"That too." He smiled at her. "And did my waiting pay off?"

Her eyes saddened for a moment, but she recovered quickly. "I told you before. I never wanted you to leave. Not then, not now."

The weight of her statement hit home, and he realised he still hadn't properly apologised for running off. Hell, for being a jerk.

He looked away, gathering his strength before facing her again. "I'm sorry."

Surprise lit her expression as she stared up at him. "Sawyer, you don't—"

"No, I do. Actually, it's long overdue." He tightened his hold on her hands. "I'm sorry, Mal. For rushing you, for not being the man you needed me to be. I should have begged for your forgiveness from the start, but instead, I took off, telling myself I was doing what was right...what was best. But it was a lie. The truth is, I wasn't brave enough to face you. To face the possibility of a life without you."

He paused, wondering what the hell she was thinking. If he was even making any sense.

He focused on her eyes, never looking away. "Leaving here allowed me to pretend there was still a chance. But the more time passed, the more I realised I'd lost any hope of getting you back. Then everything changed, and I found myself standing before you, wishing I'd never left. If I have one regret, it's not staying to find out why you'd changed your mind. Hell, it was the least I could have done...should've done."

He inched forward, praying the tears gathering in her eyes were out of love, not regret. "I can't undo the last two years, and maybe it's best if we don't even try. I know I have a long way to go before earning your trust back, but if you're willing, I'd like to spend the rest of my life trying." He squeezed her hands once. "And maybe, when you're ready, we could give the whole husband and wife thing another go-round."

Mallory stared at him, her glassy eyes wide, her breath seemingly lodged in her chest. She appeared frozen until the touch of a smile curved one side of her mouth. She moved in and dropped a sweet kiss on his mouth. "I like the sound of that."

A warm feeling spread through his chest, easing a tension he hadn't realised had taken root. He pulled her close, wondering if they should just skip the shower and head straight to bed. After everything that had happened, he couldn't think of a better ending than holding her close as she slept in his arms.

Mallory snuggled into his chest, moulding her lithe body to his. Damn, she felt good.

She chuckled when he started to move them towards the bed and eased back, tsking as she shook a finger at him. "You said something about a warm shower, first."

"Wouldn't you rather just snuggle in bed?"

Love sparkled in her eyes, followed closely by desire. "Why limit myself to only one option when you've already promised me both?"

"You're dangerous, you know that?"

"It's been mentioned before." She tugged him in the direction of the bathroom, holding his hand as they walked through the doorway and over to the shower. Her eyes never left his as she opened the door and swivelled the knobs, the patter of water echoing through the room. Her gaze drifted the length of his body, the lust in them impossible to miss, before locking on his again. She finally released his hand and smoothed her fingers down his shirt, pausing when they were fisted around the hem. The tentative smile spread into a stunning curl of her lips as she lifted his shirt over his head, allowing it to fall to the floor. Her hands skimmed over his abdomen and ribs until she palmed his chest. "And for the record, we never technically stopped being husband and wife."

Then her lips found his, the kiss equal parts desperation and need. He wrapped his arms around her, crushing her against his chest. Her nipples poked his ribs, the hard points begging to be consumed. He tried to reach for her shirt, but she ended the kiss, shaking her head as she went to her knees. Her gaze was dark, intense, and he knew he'd give her anything just to ease the burden she insisted on carrying.

Shaking fingers thumbed the band of his pants, circling his hips until they met in the middle, the smooth feel of her nails caressing his skin. She didn't rush, taking her time to slowly pop his button free and ease the edges of the material apart. A hushed hum of approval drifted across the short distance and she paused to draw small patterns on the inch of skin she'd revealed.

Sawyer set his jaw, willing his dick to stand down. The last thing she needed was him coming all over her hand before she'd even taken the damn thing out of his pants. But God, just thinking about her placing her soft lips around his shaft before sucking him deep made his balls tingle.

He took a deep breath, concentrating on anything but the hiss of the zipper as she lowered it, nipping at his cock through his briefs. The head pulsed, and he knew there'd be a wet mark to accentuate his condition.

Mallory moved up and down his length as she tugged on his pants, finally pulling them and his shorts over his hips. She released him just long enough to spring his cock free before licking a long line up to the tip, the breadth of her tongue lapping at the drop of pre-cum gleaming on the head. His pants dropped to the floor, and she paused to push one foot free. The remaining fabric hit the floor, the sound dulled by the throbbing of his pulse in his head. He reached for her just as she slipped her lips around his cock and took his length deep to the back of her throat.

"Fuck. Darling." He gathered her hair in his hands, keeping it back from her face as she moved along him, the sight of her mouth wrapped around his dick just as hot as the act itself. His gaze fell to her groin and he wished he'd taken the time to strip her down.

"You know, this would be even better if I could see how wet you were."

She glanced up at him, the edges of her mouth tightening into what he knew was a smile. She kept her gaze locked on his as she drew back until just the head was sealed inside her mouth, then she shrugged and surged towards him, sucking on him until he thought his eyes would bulge out.

"Tease. You're not going to show me anything, are you?"

She eased him free. "Patience."

He cursed as she nipped her way down his cock to nuzzle his balls, gently sucking each one into her mouth. Fire tingled along his spine, threatening to end her seduction before it'd truly begun. He closed his eyes, willing for some semblance of control as her tongue returned to his shaft, flicking up and down it with lazy strokes. Heat flared along his skin with every touch and he had to fight to keep from fisting her hair.

Mallory hummed again, adding another layer of sensation. The tiny vibrations skittered along his shaft, mixing with the warm feel of her mouth. He groaned and dropped his head, finally opening his eyes to gaze at her. Bright blue stared back at him, her long lashes veiling part of her eyes in shadows.

"God, you're beautiful." He tugged on her hair. "Come on. My turn."

She chuckled around his cock, shaking her head as she increased her rhythm, plunging deep then quickly retreating. The increased pressure tensed the muscles in his thighs and gut, and he knew he wouldn't last much longer. She was too good, too right.

A scratch of her nails along his stomach unhinged him, and he started thrusting, trusting her to meter his movements. She raised one hand to cup his cock, holding it perfectly for him to move freely. She didn't try to take control, allowing him to set the pace as her other hand teased his sac.

"Damn, darling. I can't hold back. If you don't want it in your mouth…"

His voice degraded into a husky moan as the tingling sensation built along the small of his back, pulsing into his groin and up his shaft. Every pass of her lips brought him closer to the edge, but he held on, not wanting the moment to be over. God, he never wanted it to end. Mallory must have sensed his impending finish, and applied more pressure, hollowing her cheeks as her teeth lightly scraped the bottom length of his shaft. The slightly rough rasp was all he needed.

"Fuck, yes."

Sawyer let his head fall back as his body tensed, his cock pulsing once before he released, his hips flexing as he emptied down her throat, each contraction sending more fire through his veins. Mallory took everything he offered, pumping his shaft when he was sure he was empty. A shudder raced through him, and he bowed over her, spent.

She purred in apparent satisfaction, still holding him in her mouth and hand until the last of his spasms subsided. Her tongue drew along his length as she slowly retreated, dropping a kiss beside the base of his cock. He managed a haggard breath as she rose from the floor, willingly moving into his embrace. Her rough panting matched his, the feel of her breath across his damp skin like pinpoints of electricity inflaming his need again.

"Wench."

She smiled against his chest. "Talk about being long overdue." She eased back, the tension finally gone from the fine creases across her forehead. "I'm betting the shower is more than hot by now."

He kicked off the other leg of his pants and stared at her. "I'm ready, but you…" He tsked at her. "If you'd been a good girl, you'd be naked, too."

"If I'd been a good girl, you wouldn't have finished in my mouth."

"Talk like that won't help you get any sleep tonight."

She shrugged. "Sleep's highly overrated." She lifted her shirt over her head, exposing her white cotton bra. "Now, I believe you promised me a shower."

Sawyer growled and lunged forward, pinning her to his chest as he ravaged her mouth. She fought just enough to make him work for his prize, delving deep inside when she finally opened her lips. Heat burned between them, and he raised his hand to flick her bra open. The tiny metal clasp separated beneath his fingers as the fabric fell apart. Warm skin met his hand as he palmed her back, kneading the firm muscles.

He pulled away, watching the thin garment slip off her shoulders and fall to the floor. "So damn pretty." He ran his fingers across the slope of her breast, his breath hitching as the nipple hardened at the gentle caress. "I could touch you all night."

She moaned as he leant forward and took the taut peak into his mouth. He flicked his tongue across the tip, pressing it against the back of his teeth. Her hand speared through his hair, burying in the length as she held him tight to her chest. He suckled her nipple, fighting against her hold enough to repeat his action on the other side. Rough breaths marked each draw on her bud, until she whispered his name, the husky need more than apparent.

Sawyer smiled and eased away, straightening up. "I love how you react to me." He thumbed her pants. "I suggest you get rid of these before I rip the fucking seams apart."

She sighed, feigning annoyance as she popped the button free and pushed the denim over her hips. He didn't miss the way her ass swayed back and forth a bit more than necessary as she inched them down, finally allowing them to pool at her feet.

He nodded at the pathetic strip of cotton covering a triangle of skin at her crotch. "Really, darling. If you're going to wear panties, shouldn't they at least look like they might cover more than a mere inch of your body?"

She shimmied her hips. "I could go without them again if you think that would be easier for you to cope with."

"How about I just tie you to the bed so I can keep you naked all the time?"

She grinned at him as she stepped towards him and pressed her body flush to his. "Oh, I can just imagine Cole's reaction when he walks in on us like that."

Sawyer growled and slipped his fingers down each side of her panties, ripping the seams before allowing the meagre scraps to fall to the floor. "Are you determined to test me tonight?" He gave her butt a light slap as he pulled them towards the shower door. "You're begging for a spanking."

"Is that a promise, *baby*?"

He clenched his jaw, moving them into the shower. She knew just how to push him to the point he lost control and took her against any handy surface, despite his best intentions to love her slowly. Softly. She didn't hide the smile gracing her lips as she stepped beneath the spray of water, the misty steam curling around her body. Water sluiced over her skin, making it glisten in the bright light. He pulled her close, attacking her mouth again before slowly turning her in his arms.

"Rest against the wall, darling."

She looked at him over her shoulder, nothing but love reflected in her eyes. God, if he'd questioned her trust in him, she'd all but showed him he'd earned it back. Tears gathered again as she did as he asked, leaning into the white tiles as the water sprayed lightly across her back.

He grabbed the soap, working the bar into a thick lather before rubbing it along her shoulders, massaging the tense muscles as he worked his way downward. A contented hum followed every swirl of his hands, her body pressing harder into the wall. He moved with her, rediscovering every inch of her body, from the lush curve of her buttocks to the delicate line of her spine. He placed his hands around her waist, palming her ribs as he snugged his chest against her back, his lips trailing along the sleek column of her neck. The small hairs prickled at the gentle contact and he couldn't stop the sudden urge to kiss the side of her jaw.

She turned towards him, her head lolling backwards against his shoulder and granting him access to the sensual hollow where her muscles threaded together. He bit the soft flesh, the primitive side of him determined to leave a mark staking his claim.

"Sawyer."

The raspy hiss of his name ignited a deeper need, and he closed his eyes as he rested his head on hers.

"God, I love you."

She stiffened slightly at his words, her sharp intake of breath revealing her thoughts before she'd even spoken them. He kissed her when she looked as if she was going to speak, loving the way she moaned into his mouth.

Their gazes locked as he finally eased back, one hand dipping down to rest on her thigh as the other angled the showerhead to rinse them off. "I don't know why you gave me a second chance, but I'm certain I don't deserve it…deserve you."

He pushed her thigh off to one side, probing her entrance with his cock. Warm moisture coated his skin and he couldn't stop from thrusting inside her, burying himself in her vise-like grip.

Mallory cried out his name, allowing him to bend her knee and wrap her heel around his back. He could tell she was off-balance, but he wouldn't let her fall. He whispered soothing words as he drew back, pausing with just the head squeezed inside her before surging back in.

"You know damn well why I gave you a second chance, and I beg to differ on your last statement." She moaned again at another pass, this one harder than before. "God, Sawyer. I need more."

"Greedy little minx, aren't you?"

He chuckled at her disgruntled huff, obliging her request. Her body shuddered with every stroke, and he knew she was already close to climaxing. He slipped his hand along her leg, cupping her mound. His fingers traced the line where they joined, and he groaned as he felt her soft flesh give to accept him.

"Damn, darling. You're so fucking hot." He slammed into her, pushing her against the tiles. "I wanted to go slow. To show you how much you mean to me, but, shit…"

He lowered his head, resting it against the base of her neck as he held her hips and pounded into her. Water splashed across her back, running in rivulets along her skin, but all he felt was her grasping channel and the hold she had over him. Her voice echoed through the small space, mixing with the steam as he worked her higher, feeling her pussy contract around him. He waited until the walls started to spasm before releasing his grasp on his control and emptying inside her.

Mallory's body went rigid, her hands fisting against the tiles. He held her close, listening to her grunt through her release before she relaxed into him, seemingly content to let him bear their weight. He smiled and wrapped one arm around her chest as the other found her waist. Her chest hit his hand with every rough inhalation, the rapid breaths mirroring his. How he'd survived two years without her was a mystery, but he knew he wouldn't last two days now. He wasn't sure if he believed in soul mates, or fate, but he knew his life meant nothing without her in it.

Mallory sighed and leaned against him. He didn't need to see her face to know she was smiling. He dropped a kiss on the top of her head, rinsing off any remaining soap before easing his weakening erection out of her. She huffed in what sounded like disappointment and turned, watching him with that slight tilt of her head that made her seem innocent and wicked all at the same time.

He cupped her chin, moving in for a soft kiss. "You're amazing. But don't think I've forgotten about that spanking."

Her smile was pure sin. "I'm counting on it." She drew her hand across his chest, lightly squeezing his flat nipples. "Now I believe you promised to be my pillow."

"I suppose I can't break a promise." He tugged her towards the door. "But remember. No snoring."

Chapter Ten

Mallory bolted awake, the soft patter of feet across the wood floors outside the bedroom jolting her from sleep. She'd heard the noise a thousand times before — had learned to recognise the tread of her father when he was on one of his benders. For a drunk, the man had been as quiet as a damn cat, and she'd become an extremely light sleeper in order to stay one step ahead of him.

Memories of those nights tumbled through her head as she stared at the door, momentarily frozen until a creak sounded from the living room. Her muscles tensed as she shuffled to the edge of the bed and quietly opened the side table drawer. Her gun felt cold and heavy in her hand as she wrapped her fingers around the handle, removing it before sliding back over. She curled her other hand around Sawyer's shoulder.

"Sawyer."

The man hummed, blinking several times as he turned to look at her. His sexy half-smile brightened the room as he reached out and caressed her arm. "In the mood again already, darling? Damn, don't you ever sleep?"

"There's someone in the house."

The lines around his mouth tightened as his gaze swung to the door, then dropped to her gun. He met her stare. "Are you sure?"

She tried not to sound too bitter. "Trust me when I tell you I'd recognise the sound of feet on a wood floor anywhere."

Sawyer's eyes narrowed and he muttered something under his breath as he rolled out of the bed, picking his jeans off the floor before tossing her his shirt. He gave her a nod as he retrieved his gun, pulled on his pants and headed for the door. Mallory followed behind him, slipping on his shirt before stopping at the closed door. Sawyer had his ear pressed against the damn thing while one hand palmed the handle. He glanced over at her and nodded.

She took a deep breath, counting with him as he reached three and opened the door, clearing up the hallway towards the living room as she slipped out behind him and cleared the path back to the spare bedroom. Eerie silence greeted them and Sawyer tapped her on the shoulder, motioning towards the spare room. She acknowledged his plan and moved down the hallway with him. While she was anxious to catch the bastard invading their home, they couldn't chance something might come at them from behind.

She stopped when they reached the room Sawyer had spent all of two hours in that first night. He pushed ahead of her, opening the door and ducking inside without a word. She cursed, but kept watch, not sure whether to be touched by his protectiveness or pissed by it. She choose the first, remembering how hurt he'd looked when he hadn't backed her up quicker in the alley.

Sawyer reappeared a few moments later, shaking his head as he nodded up the corridor. She took off, clearing the bathroom before continuing towards the living room. Sawyer took point, keeping his back to the wall as he stared into the darkness. Mallory took the other side, her gun nestled beside her shoulder. They counted to three then shifted out, each taking a side. A cool breeze coasted along the floor, swirling around her feet. They moved as one, clearing the living room then moving to the kitchen. Sawyer searched every closet, every possible hiding spot before finally addressing the open front door. Though she was certain he'd locked it after they'd arrived home, it stood wedged against the wall, nothing but darkness beyond the entryway.

He cursed and kicked the thing shut, obviously not wanting to risk touching it without gloves. She relaxed slightly when he flicked on the lights, bathing the room in a harsh light.

He ran a clenched hand through his hair. "What the fuck? I know I locked the damn door, and not just the handle. I used the deadbolt."

"No lock is impenetrable. Hell, I picked harder doors than that in foster care."

He gave her a hardened look. "That's not the kind of shit I want to hear right now. Not when you've been living here, alone, for the last two years." He held up his hand to stop further comments. "I know. I'm to blame for that. Just humour me right now, okay?"

She smiled and moved into his open arms. "It wasn't just you, and I can assure you I'm not an easy target. But we should see if anything's missing."

Sawyer sighed. "I can't believe someone would be stupid enough to break into our house. Shit, what were they thinking? If we'd caught them…"

Mallory nodded, following him through the kitchen and into the living room. She squinted as Sawyer flicked on the lights, blinking at the sudden glare. Nothing seemed out of place until she swung her gaze towards the bar. A small blanket was mounded on the counter, the edge of a knitted foot sticking out of one end.

Sawyer glanced at her, his eyebrow raised in question. "What the hell is that?"

"Not sure I want to know." She moved beside him. "Do you want to do the honours, or should I?"

"Just stay back."

He walked across the room, stopping an arm's length away. He glanced back at her then grabbed one end, keeping his fingers near the edge. Mallory held her breath as he gently lifted the fabric, pausing halfway to look underneath. His loud curse made her jump as he snatched the blanket away, tossing it off to the side. She inched forward, unable to distinguish what the lump was until she got a few feet away. She inhaled roughly, staring at the old knitted doll with a manila envelope tied to the front with a sash. More memories tumbled through her head and she looked away, all too sure what was inside the beige offering.

* * * *

Sawyer opened the door, trying not to scowl at the man standing on the porch. A passing car cast a long shadow along the driveway, reminding him it wasn't even three o'clock yet. Mallory stepped up beside him, elbowing him in the ribs as she smiled at the man.

"Fisher. Thanks for coming. I know it's late, it's just..." She sighed, motioning him inside.

Fisher gave her a smile, picking up his case as he stepped through the doorway. "It's okay. I'd just gotten home, anyway." He extended his hand to Sawyer. "I'd heard you were back in town. Good to see you." He winked at Mallory. "I'd also heard Sawyer's been staying in your spare room without bloodshed. Are you sure you're feeling okay?"

Mallory laughed, though it sounded tight. "The case isn't over, yet. Maybe I'm just lulling everyone into a false sense of security, so I won't be the prime suspect when Sawyer goes missing."

Fisher chuckled. "That sounds more like the Mallory I know." He paused as he glanced at the next room. "Is it in there?"

Sawyer moved in behind Mallory, not sure whether to hold her shoulders or stay at a distance. Though he was certain Fisher had guessed at their current sleeping arrangements, joking aside, he didn't want to put any pressure on Mallory. She'd more than stepped up for him, and he needed to give her all the time she required before making their renewed relationship common knowledge.

He brushed her hand then nodded at Fisher. "All I did was remove the blanket. Otherwise, we haven't touched it."

Fisher headed for the living room, glancing down the hallway before going straight for the bar. The doll still rested on the counter, the dull, grey fabric of the blanket heaped beside it. Fisher didn't speak, just put down the case, pulled out his camera and started snapping photographs.

Sawyer watched him work, keeping an eye on Mallory. She hadn't said much since he'd uncovered the doll, and he knew there was more to the offering than just the envelope. Dread settled in his gut. He had a bad feeling he knew what was inside.

Fisher straightened as he let the camera rest against his chest. He turned back to them, an apologetic half-smile curling his mouth. "I assume you've both noticed the detail in the setup—the way the sash is tied identical to all of Davies' victims not to mention the drawn-on markings on the neck, wrists and ankles of the doll."

"It was hard to miss." Sawyer crossed his arms on his chest. "Though I don't know why he picked a doll, not that I'm complaining. I half expected a severed head."

Fisher cracked a slight grin, nodding at him. He looked at Mallory. "Any insight on the doll, Mal?"

Sawyer glanced at her, the sudden silence sending a cold shiver down his spine. *Shit*. He should have guessed the doll hadn't just been a convenient medium for Davies to convey his message. He inched closer, palming the middle of her back when she sighed and toed at the floor.

"The doll was mine."

"What?" Sawyer spun her around. "What the hell do you mean the doll was yours? From when?"

She held up her hand, looking them both in the eye before continuing. "I don't mean it's actually my doll, at least, I don't think it is, it's just…I had one. Identical to it when I was little, before…" She paused, glancing at Fisher before sighing and running a shaky hand through her hair. "Fuck. Why does it always come back to that night?" She huffed. "Long story short, Fisher—my father was a drunken wife-beater and my mother saw fit to finally deal with it by sticking a knife in him. Several times. And that…" She pointed at the doll. "Was all that kept me sane most nights. But I haven't seen it since the cops dragged me out of that house."

Sawyer tensed his jaw. He'd kill Davies or whoever was tormenting Mallory and he'd enjoy every fucking second of it. He laid his hand on her shoulder, but she simply shrugged and wrapped her arms protectively around her chest.

"I don't know how Davies or his partner would know that. Hell of a lucky guess if you ask me."

"We both know luck isn't in this equation." Sawyer met Fisher's gaze. "Any thoughts?"

Fisher snorted. "Yeah, that whoever's doing this is one sick bastard and the city would sleep far better if one of you put a bullet in his head."

Sawyer grinned. "I'll see what I can do."

Fisher gave him a smile, patting Mallory on her other shoulder again before looking at the doll. He smile faded into a frown. "I'm going to go out on a limb here and guess that the envelope contains pictures, not some cryptic note."

Sawyer clenched his jaw. "I'd say that's an accurate assumption."

Fisher nodded then glanced from the envelope back to them. He took a deep breath, shifting a bit on his feet before exhaling loudly. "Look, I think it's safe to say that there are two possibilities here. Either the bastard has sent us detailed images of the crimes scenes, or..."

When he left the thought hanging, Sawyer raised one eyebrow. "Or?"

Fisher glanced at the hallway. "I'm more than aware of your guys' history...including the personal side. So if these aren't crime scene photos, I'm betting you've spent very little time in that spare room, the proof of which is chronicled inside this envelope." He held up his hand to stop Sawyer from talking. "Yeah. I know. It could be a thousand other kinds of photos, but let's face it. Pictures of the two of you would be the most damning, at least in a killer's eyes, especially since your relationship is still somewhat guarded."

Sawyer didn't chance a gaze at Mallory, afraid his possessive side would surge forward and he'd puff up his chest like some primitive Neanderthal, professing ownership of his woman. Instead, he kept his expression fixed as he faced Fisher. "Somehow, I don't think our guy broke in here just to leave some gory photos behind."

Fisher nodded. "I have extra gloves. If you two would like to look at these privately —"

"Why?" Mallory stepped forward. "Even if there are personal images in there, it's not like we can just discard them. They're evidence...however revealing they might be." She gave Sawyer a slight smile. "I just hope he got my good side."

Sawyer reached for her hand, giving it a squeeze. "That would imply you have a bad one, darling."

Fisher cleared his throat. "Should I leave for a bit?"

Sawyer scoffed and shook his head. "Just open the damn envelope."

Fisher chuckled and turned to the bar. He undid the sash, pausing to take more close ups as he went. By the time he slid the flap open, Sawyer's heart rate had tripled. While the thought of seeing Mallory in all her glory was alluring, these weren't the circumstances he'd envisioned. And the idea that some creep had been stalking them — stalking her — boiled his blood.

Fisher backed up, holding the envelope so they could all see. "Ready?"

He didn't wait for an answer, just eased his hand inside and removed a set of prints. Sawyer studied the first one, not familiar with the surroundings.

Fisher sucked in a quick breath. "That's from the first crime scene, shortly after you and Cole arrived. I believe the bastard in question hadn't been dead more than a few hours at that point."

"Anyone could have taken the photos," said Mallory. "Or maybe someone set up a hidden camera. He could have hundreds of pictures from that night."

"Whatever it is, it's bloody creepy." Fisher shuffled through a couple more, stopping at the next change of venue. He held it up to them.

"Shit. That's the alleyway." Sawyer leaned in closer. "How the hell did he get one in there when he was in front of us?" He fisted one hand at the next photo, looking at Mallory. "He got one of you fighting?"

He reached for the picture when Mallory grabbed his hand.

"Easy, Sawyer."

He growled inwardly but pulled his hand back.

Fisher flipped to the next. "The bar. That I'd recognise anywhere." He glanced at Sawyer then winked at Mallory. "Nice shiner. I bet Sawyer went ballistic over that one."

She smiled. "He's still touchy."

"You both know I'm standing right here."

Fisher chuckled, shuffling again, when Sawyer's breath hitched. They were in the Jeep, Mallory's sexy body on top of his. He could see the white of her lace bra and the creamy line of her hips brushed against the steering wheel. The only blemish was a single, bloody fingerprint dried onto the lower portion of the photo.

To Fisher's credit, the man didn't do more than arch an eyebrow before shifting his gaze to the fingerprint. He lifted the photo, taking a closer look at the raised ridges and swirls. "I'm thinking we all know whose print this is. But nice of him to leave me such a clean one." He flipped to the next picture. "Got another one. Looks like a different finger, though."

Sawyer didn't hold back his growl this time. Another photo of Mallory, only this time her head was thrown back towards the windshield as he kissed the sleek column of her throat, nothing between them but the moonlight. "Goddamn."

Mallory hit him in the shoulder, glaring at him. "At least it's not your ass on display, or anything else, really, for that matter."

"Darling…"

She held up her hand. "Don't." She sighed. "And it's not that my ass is on display. It's just… Fuck. The creep was watching us. The entire time." She cringed when a picture of Sawyer carrying her inside, her body naked against his, surfaced next. "Seriously?"

Fisher cleared his throat, glancing at both of them. "If it's any consolation, I promise I'll be as discreet as possible."

Sawyer paced across the room, wishing he'd grabbed a whisky before Fisher had arrived. "I doubt it's a coincidence that the only photos with fingerprints on them are the ones of us, together."

"Probably not, but…" Fisher paused. "Look. It's not like most of us didn't think you two were doing the nasty, so this isn't all that shocking. Hell, there were even rumours going around that you guys had tied the knot." He held up the collection of photos. "I'll just keep these well protected until I'm finished processing them, then we'll hide them away in an evidence bag. Very few people really need to see these."

Mallory groaned, looking as if she wished the floor would open up and swallow her. "It's not people knowing about us that's the issue. It's knowing he's been watching us…all the time. Everywhere. First the alley, then my old house and now this! What the fuck is up with this guy?"

Sawyer cursed and moved over to her, pushing his chest against her back. He wasn't sure whether she'd pull away and all but moaned when she leaned against him, releasing a heavy breath as he wrapped one arm around her shoulder and across her upper chest, allowing the other to rest on her hip. God, she felt good in his arms.

He pushed his chin against the side of her neck. "We'll get him. Making this personal was a huge mistake, one that will haunt him. It's only a matter of time before he does something he can't recover from."

She kissed his arm. "I'm free tomorrow if you'd like to catch his creepy ass."

He chuckled. "Maybe Fisher can give us some good news by then."

Fisher sighed. "I'll do my best, but the photos look pretty clean, other than the obvious prints. But you never know." He placed them back in the envelope. "I'll get to them first thing—run the prints, see if the bastard left anything else. I should have something for you by noon."

Sawyer nodded. "Thanks. We owe you."

"No problem. What are friends for if you can't call them out at three a.m?" He bagged the evidence and packed up his case then headed for the door, pausing at the threshold. "But in the spirit of giving, I gotta know...just between us. Did you guys really get married?"

Sawyer tensed, not sure how to respond when Mallory looked at him across her shoulder, a smile lighting up her entire face.

She gave him a wink then turned to Fisher. "Yeah. We really did."

Fisher hooted and pumped his fist in the air. "I knew it." He opened the door but stopped again and glanced back. "Are you still married?"

Sawyer welcomed the weight of her body as she leaned into him again, her hand lifting to cover his. It was the first time someone other than Cole had even mentioned it.

She laughed as she gazed up at him again, seemingly obvious to the fact Fisher was standing there, waiting. "Yup. We still are."

Fisher smiled, and headed out, calling back over his shoulder. "I'm so winning the pool when you guys finally come out."

Sawyer chuckled then sobered. "Wait! There's a pool for that? Fisher!"

Mallory grabbed his arm as he tried to follow the man out the door.

She shook her head and closed it behind him, twining her fingers through his and tugging him towards the bedroom. "Of course there's a pool. I took tomorrow at ten o'clock for when Cole stumbles back in."

"Really? I took eleven. The man likes to sleep in a bit."

She smiled again, and his heart dropped. God, she was just too beautiful when she smiled.

He stopped and pulled her into his chest. "You know you just blew our cover, right?"

"Those pictures blew our cover, not that we had very much of one. You heard Fisher. Everyone already knows. They're just waiting on an official confirmation."

"Which you pretty much gave."

Her lips quirked up at one side. "Nervous of the truth getting out, *darling*?"

"You're kidding, right? I had a neon sign made for just this occasion." He eased away backing up towards the bedroom again. "Come on. I promised you I'd be your pillow for the night and I don't want to break any more promises."

Chapter Eleven

"Jesus Christ, Mal. I'm not here for a few hours and all hell breaks loose."

Mallory looked up from the paperwork stacked on her desk as Cole shuffled to a halt, his left arm bound in a sling, his right stuffed in his jeans' pocket. Dark smudges lined the bottom of his eyes, and his mouth was pulled tight at the corners.

She glanced at the clock, cursing under her breath. "Good morning to you, too."

"Screw the pleasantries. Why the hell didn't you call me last night?"

She snorted and leant back in her chair. "It was three o'clock in the morning. You were in the hospital, which reminds me. Shouldn't you still be there? I'm pretty damn sure I heard the doctor say something about twenty-four hours."

He glared at her. "You're the last person to preach about following orders. Besides, having the prime suspect of an ongoing serial murder investigation break into your house pretty much supersedes everything else. As it was, I didn't know shit until

Fisher called to ask me something about one of the photos."

"I was going to tell you just as soon as you showed up, which I thought would be about an hour ago, by the way."

Cole drew his brows together just as Sawyer tapped him on the shoulder. Cole turned, staring at Sawyer as the man handed him a coffee.

He nodded at Cole. "Actually, you're right on time. Eleven even." Sawyer flashed a smile at Mallory. "Told you he likes to sleep in."

Cole stared at him as he walked past Mallory and sat down, crossing his feet at the ankles.

Mallory chuckled. "Come on, Cole. We both knew you wouldn't stay. In fact, everyone knew you wouldn't stay. Unfortunately, I took ten o'clock." She motioned to Sawyer. "He took eleven."

"Which means I win the pool."

Mallory turned to him. "Feel free to stop gloating any time now."

Cole held up his hand, stopping the conversation. "I'm not even gone twenty-four hours and you guys have a pool going? Damn, that was quick."

Mallory outright laughed. "You know how much Fisher likes the chance at beating all of our asses. Speaking of which, did you enter the one on when Sawyer and I would come out for good?"

"No. Seeing as I had inside information, I chose not to. Besides, Fisher already had the spot I wanted." Cole cursed then glanced at the coffee. He gawked at Sawyer. "I can't believe you brought me coffee. That's pretty smug."

Sawyer shrugged. "Mallory isn't the only one who knows you, buddy, which is why I just won the pool."

Cole released a weary breath. "Fuck. We are some kind of weird threesome."

Mallory patted his thigh as he rested one hip on her desk. "You can sleep in the middle if it makes you feel any better about it."

"Very funny." He dropped his gaze to a manila envelope on her desk. "So are those the photos Fisher was asking about?"

She clenched her jaw but nodded. No sense worrying about Cole seeing the images, not when he'd already walked in on her and Sawyer. She grabbed the envelope and handed it to him. "Fisher ran a bunch of tests, but the bastard didn't leave anything other than the obvious prints."

Cole opened the flap and removed the pictures. "I assume they belong to Davies."

"A positive match. Blood, too."

"Fantastic."

She watched Cole as he flipped through the images, studying some before going to the next. She knew the moment he'd stumbled upon the photos of her and Sawyer. His eyes bulged wide and he swung his gaze towards Sawyer before meeting hers. She gave him a tight smile, not daring to look at Sawyer. With the way he'd been acting lately, she wouldn't be surprised if he jumped up and started pounding his chest as he strutted around the desks.

Cole tsked as he shook one of the pictures. "The Jeep? Damn, I have to ride in that car, you know."

Mallory shrugged it off as best she could. "I have to ride in your truck, and I know the inside of that thing has seen more action than *G.I. Joe*."

"Now you're just being nasty because someone caught you doing some sort of sexual yoga with lover boy over there." His face lit into a wide grin. "How the hell did you manage not to throw your back out?" He held up his hand when she opened her mouth. "Don't bother. After all I've seen with you two, nothing surprises me." He shuffled again and laughed. "You should really go to a tanning salon, Mal. Your ass is pasty white."

Mallory grabbed her water bottle and gave Cole a mock toss.

He laughed as he swatted her in the shoulder, motioning to the disk on her desk. "What's that?" He grinned. "Don't tell me Davies got movies, too."

She sneered at him, trying not to smile. Damn but the man was more trouble than Sawyer at times. She held it up. "Actually, it's the footage of the execution. The penitentiary had it couriered over. Sawyer thought we might see something useful on it."

Cole frowned. "Not that it isn't a great idea, it's just… You up for that?"

"I'll give it the college try, but no promises."

Sawyer scraped his chair closer. "Cole and I can watch it. There's no reason to upset you."

She sighed, hating that she was so transparent to him—hell, both of them. "It's not that it upsets me, but… Shit. I wish I knew what it was about Davies that creeped me out so much, besides the obvious stabbing incident. There's just something about him." She shivered. "I can watch at least as far as we got before my phone rang."

Sawyer nodded, staying conspicuously close. The simple gesture sent heat spiralling through her body and she had to look away from Cole before the flush in her cheeks betrayed her feelings.

Cole dragged another chair over as Sawyer slipped the disk into the computer, launching the movie once it was loaded. There was a burst of static and white light before the room morphed into view on the screen, the thick glass centred in the frame. The curtains were still closed as people moved about the room, changing seats and talking quietly. The hushed murmurs played in the background until the screech of the curtains rang out, plunging the room into a deadly quiet.

A couple more people walked in front of the lens before the doors on the other side of the glass opened, and Davies entered, his head held high, his thin lips pulled back into a snarl. Just staring at him made her feel light-headed. Damn, that was the same face she'd seen in the alleyway and just thinking he might still be alive curdled her blood.

The scene played on, and she watched as Davies was escorted to the gurney and strapped down. This was where she'd ditched the proceedings the first time. Emotions warred inside her as they had that night, and she had to consciously slow her breathing to keep the room from dimming at the edges. Sawyer's hand cupped hers and she glanced at him, not even bothering to hide the fear roiling through her. He gave her a sincere smile and motioned at the break room.

She sighed but nodded, knowing she wouldn't be any help at this point. She twisted around, giving the computer one last passing glance before stopping dead. "Wait!" She hit the space bar, freezing the DVD.

Cole leant forward, giving her a concerned raise of his eyebrow. "Mal? You okay?"

She grabbed the mouse and popped up the controls, reversing the footage. "Did you see it?"

He snorted. "See what? All I see is Davies and his creepy grin."

She shook her head, slowly playing the movie forward frame by frame. "No. The reflection in the glass of one of the guards. God, it can't be." She advanced a few more times before drawing a sharp breath as she stared at the image on the screen.

Sawyer's head appeared beside her as he leaned in. "Is it my imagination or does that guy's face look very familiar?"

Cole whistled as he touched the screen. "I'll be damned. That's Carter." He hit a few keys, enlarging the image. "The image is pretty grainy, and he's changed his appearance somewhat, but that's definitely Derek Carter."

Mallory pushed to her feet. "How the hell did Derek Carter get inside the room? Christ, he's wearing a guard's uniform!"

Cole slipped out his cell as he punched some numbers. "No fucking idea, but I intend to find out." He moved away, talking sternly into the phone.

Mallory stared at the picture, jumping when Sawyer touched her sleeve. She turned, nearly bumping into his chest. Her gaze swept the room, but no one seemed to be interested in why he was standing so close to her. She gave him a nod, but he held his ground. "Sawyer —"

"I'll back up when you tell me why you didn't call me and ask me to be there that night."

She drew her brows together. "What?"

He pointed at the screen. "Why the hell didn't you call me and tell me how hard it was going to be for you? Hell, I would have come, awkward or not." He slapped a fist against his thigh. "I knew you'd be uncomfortable, but I never guessed it was this bad." He gave her a stern shake of his finger. "You should have called me."

"You were requested by Washington to attend. I thought that might be enough."

He ran his hand through his hair, looking as if he wanted to pull some out. "I don't give a shit about Washington. But I would have come for you...no questions asked."

She sighed. "You're here now. Isn't that what matters?"

"Are you sure that's enough? I know you've said you forgive me, but... Damn, Mal. Davies and now it seems that Carter might be involved. This is way beyond anything I ever imagined. If there's even a chance that creep is alive..."

"You said it yourself. It's highly unlikely. Even if Carter is in on this and he managed to bribe the doctor into pronouncing Davies dead, there're a thousand other details that could have blown up in his face before he actually got Davies out of there...alive. More likely Carter's the guy sending us everything. Now we just have to figure out why and where Davies fits into it, if he even does." She took another quick look around before tiptoeing up and giving him a quick kiss. "And you are forgiven. Just say the word and I'll walk into Don's office and tell him everything, though he mostly knows already."

Sawyer released a harsh breath and stepped back. "I just hate watching you hurt like this. Damn good thing your father is dead because I'd be paying him a visit otherwise."

She smiled. "One small mercy, I suppose. And you can take your frustrations out on the creep behind all this once we find him." She pointed at Don's office. "Should I go say hello to the Director now?"

"We'll do it together...after we crack this case. I don't want to take any chances he might reassign me before that happens."

"Fair enough. And for the record, I wanted to call. I was just too chickenshit to finish dialling." She gave his hand a squeeze. "But I wouldn't hesitate now, not that I plan on letting you get away from me again."

"Oh for the love of God, would you two just get a room before someone else gets you both on film?" Cole shouldered up beside them. "Seriously. I might need to go back to the hospital if you start giving each other goo-goo eyes."

Mallory hit his good shoulder. "Fuck you."

"You keep saying it but you never come through."

She rolled her eyes. "And you're an ass. Now tell me you got something useful."

Cole grimaced and held up a picture. "I got something, but it's just more bad news. I'd like you both to meet Corrections Officer James Reeves."

Mallory gasped. "Who?"

Cole nodded. "I know. Just another blow to you that he used your father's name. Actually, according to the file they just sent me, he used a bunch of your father's personal information—his birthday, that old house address. Hell, he even fabricated a fake family with the same names." He eyed Mallory. "You look pretty sophisticated for a ten-year-old."

"This just keeps getting stranger and stranger. I'd never really met Carter until we worked the Davies case together. How can he know all of this?"

Sawyer held up his phone, her father's information glaring back at her. "If the guy can create false IDs, I bet my ass he can access old police files. Even if he can't, there are more public records than you'd think. Everything he needs to know is out there. Shit, it only took me a minute to get this."

"But why? What am I to him?"

"Maybe he had a crush on you and didn't take it well when Sawyer moved in on what he considered his territory."

"I barely saw the guy. How the hell was I ever his territory?"

Cole shrugged. "The guy's obviously a nut job. I don't think things need to be rational in our terms to make sense to him. But figuring out why might be the break we've been hoping for. He's made this personal. That's what we need to explore."

Mallory palmed her head when her cell rang, the steady beat of the music filling the sudden quiet. She groaned inwardly as she reached in her pocket, lifting the phone out and swiping the smooth surface. "Reeves."

A heavy breath rasped in her ear, followed by a dark chuckle. "Hello, Agent Reeves. Have you missed me?"

Mallory tensed, glancing at Sawyer before forcing herself to swallow. "Davies. Didn't know they had phones in Hell. The long distance rates must be a killer."

"Clever, aren't you? If only this case was that simple, you'd have solved it by now instead of waiting for more victims so you can get the answers to all of your questions, though I've already given you four plus Mr Thomas. I'd have thought you'd have some by now."

"I'm working on it. But I am starting to think that the rumours regarding your death are highly exaggerated."

He laughed. "You might have guessed at that if you'd bothered to stay that night. Shame you had to run off before it really got started."

"It's okay. I'll catch the next one."

"There won't be a next one. I believe I told you at our last meeting that you couldn't kill me."

"You probably did. But I'm fairly certain I can pay someone to drag your sick soul back to Hell."

"That's what I like about you, Agent Reeves. Always looking at the positive side of things." He cleared his throat. "I see Agent Kent is back in town, not to mention your bed. You must be very happy."

The mention of Sawyer's name made her stomach flip-flop and she had to clench her jaw to keep from tossing her breakfast across her desk. She glanced at Sawyer as he hovered beside her ear, trying to hear every word.

She took a deep breath. "You should have stayed longer at the house. I'm sure he would have enjoyed saying hello in person."

"Perhaps another time. But I'm sure I'll be seeing you both soon. After all, you are tracing the call, aren't you?"

"Standard protocol, as you're obviously aware of. Though you could save me the trouble of talking with dispatch and just tell me where you are."

He laughed again, the sound just as nauseating as before. "And spoil all the fun of working it out? I wouldn't dream of it. How's Cole's shoulder?"

"Healing. He's standing right here. Would you like to talk to him?"

"I think we both know I only called to talk to you. It's always been about you."

"I'm starting to get that impression. Don't suppose you'd agree to a meeting? Just you and me?"

Sawyer growled under his breath as his hand curled around her arm. She didn't need to look at him to know there wasn't a chance in Hell he'd ever agree to that, but then she didn't think Davies would, either.

"A nice offer, but I'll have to turn you down this time. But soon, I promise." He released another raspy breath. "Until next time, Agent Reeves."

The phone clicked and went dead, the eerie silence more sickening than his voice had been. She closed her eyes as she lowered the phone, praying her hands weren't shaking as much as she thought. God, what was it about that man that got to her? That turned her back into the scared little girl hiding under her bed?

A strong hand closed over her shoulder and she jumped, opening her eyes as she stared into Sawyer's handsome face. His eyes were narrowed and the edges of his mouth were turned down into the beginning of a frown.

He gave her a gentle squeeze. "You okay?"

She nodded, knowing her voice would confirm the worry she saw creasing his forehead. He seemed to study her face for a moment before sighing and straightening, turning to Cole. The man was talking on his cell and gave them the signal to hold on.

Mallory chewed at her bottom lip, trying to reconstruct the conversation in her head. There had to be a specific reason he'd called, a reason he wanted them to track his location. But it went completely against his profile.

Sawyer moved in front of her. "Let's hope dispatch was able to pinpoint his location. Too damn bad he called on your cell. No way to record the conversation and run it through voice analysis. I'm sure that was his intent." He leaned in closer. "Could you tell if that was really Davies on the phone?"

"It sure sounded like him, but... Shit. I haven't heard the creep talk in over a year. I'd have to listen to voice comparisons to be certain. It could be someone trying to sound like him."

"Damn. I was hoping we could narrow things down a bit."

"All I know is that it didn't sound like Carter that I remember. But again, I haven't seen him since the case was closed, either."

"Go over everything he said. Was any of it unusual? Maybe something Davies wouldn't have said?"

Mallory reran the conversation again when something struck her as odd. "Wait. He called me Agent Reeves."

Sawyer frowned. "So?"

"He always called me Mallory, as if calling me by my first name made the killings more intimate or something. He never did say."

Sawyer pursed his lips. "Maybe—"

He cut off as Cole muttered a goodbye into his phone and lowered it, his expression more sombre than she'd expected.

Dread tumbled through Mallory's gut and she braced herself for more bad news. "Just tell us, already."

Cole shuffled on his feet. "Dispatch traced the call, but…"

"But what? Where is the bastard?"

Cole steeled his expression. "He's calling from Gig Harbor."

Sawyer furrowed his brow. "What the hell is he doing in Gig Harbor and why would he want us to know…" His expression changed. "Shit."

Mallory stood there, staring at him when it hit her. "The women's correctional centre is in Gig Harbor." She inhaled roughly. "My mother."

Cole grabbed her as she tried to push past him. "They've already notified the superintendent. They're doing a lockdown and checking everyone as we speak."

"I'm still going. She might not consider me her daughter, but she's still my mother."

"Of course you are, but we're coming and Sawyer's driving."

She palmed the desk for support as fear swept over her. "God. I haven't seen her since…"

"Mal—"

Mallory glared at him, pushing off. "I'm fine, Cole."

"No, you're not. And you'll be less fine in forty-five minutes when we get there. So we're playing this my way, end of discussion."

"Fine." She pulled her arm free and grabbed her jacket, not meeting either of the men's gazes as she headed for the elevators, tossing Sawyer the keys to the Jeep back over her shoulder. She had a bad feeling Davies had just changed the nature of his game, and it was more personal than ever.

Chapter Twelve

"Goddamn, son of a bitch."

Sawyer slammed his hand on the wall as he stared into the small cell, noting the increasing pool of blood spreading across the floor. He'd made the drive in under hour, but it hadn't been fast enough. The superintendent had met them at the door, her mouth a thin line across her face as she'd lowered her head and informed them Pamela Reeves was dead.

Mallory hadn't spoken a word, choosing to follow the woman through the bowels of the facility in complete silence until they arrived at Pam's unit. The door had been left open and the body perfectly arranged on the floor. The only deviation was a photo of Mallory pinned to her mother's sash.

Cole came up beside him and gave him a nod. "This is insane. What the hell have we stumbled into? This isn't the work of a typical serial killer. Shit, this guy doesn't have a MO anymore. All he seems to want to do is make Mallory suffer."

"I can assure you, he's succeeding."

Cole sighed. "You think she'll be okay?" He cursed. "You know what I mean, Sawyer. She's not going to be good, but…should I be worried?"

"Honestly, I don't know. But I wouldn't suggest leaving her alone…not even for a moment."

"Just don't ask me to follow her into the ladies' room. I like my balls attached to my body if it's all the same to you."

Sawyer smiled in spite of himself. "She's lucky to have a friend like you. You know that, right? Hell, we both are."

"Thanks." Cole gave him a cautious nod. "We don't have to hug or anything now, do we?"

"Not if you're as attached to your balls as much as you say you are." He released a slow breath. "None of this makes sense. All the other victims were young women. And why kill someone who's destined to spend the rest of their life behind bars? I get he's making a statement, but… Shit. I don't have a clue what he's trying to tell us."

"Maybe the message isn't for us."

Sawyer turned to Cole just as Mallory walked out of the cell. He gave Cole a nod then met her halfway, not sure what to expect. She looked up at him all glassy-eyed and lost and his instincts took over. He opened his arms and pulled her tight to his chest, muffling her gasp of surprise. She remained stiff for a moment before melting against him, a rough sob breaking free. He closed his eyes, using one hand to stroke her hair as the other held her firm. He didn't care about appearances or protocol. All he cared about was soothing the hurt, even if only for a few minutes.

Mallory took a few shuddering breaths, staying encased in his arms for a couple of minutes before finally pushing against him. Her eyes were still brimming with unshed tears when she eased away, crossing her arms around her chest as they broke contact. He gave her a tilt of his head, silently telling her he didn't give a shit who was watching, but she shook her head, offering him a small smile as she released a heavy sigh.

She looked over at Cole. "Did you call Fisher?"

"He should be here any minute." Cole clenched his jaw. "He'll need to know if you…"

Mallory nodded as his voice trailed off. "I didn't touch anything. I just needed…"

Cole stepped forward. "Mallory."

She held up a hand. "It's okay. We weren't exactly close."

"Close or not, I know you loved her, if for nothing else than for saving you that night. This isn't Don or the Bureau psychologist. It's us. You don't have to put up some façade because you're afraid we'll think you're weak."

Her eyes widened slightly, releasing a few of the tears. Sawyer had to fist his hands at his side to keep from pulling her close again as the shiny drops chased each other down her skin, falling like broken glass to the floor.

She swung her gaze to him, but it only made her look more defeated. "Maybe I just don't have any more tears to cry for her, at least not the kind you're thinking of." She glanced back into the cell. "But regardless of what she'd become—what we'd become—she didn't deserve this. Not this." She looked at Cole. "I want this guy. I want…"

Sawyer stared at her, waiting for her to finish her thought when she drew a deep breath.

She glanced down the hallway then back at them. "The photos."

Sawyer arched one brow. "What about the photos?"

"He's taken them at every crime scene. Do you honestly think he'd go to all this trouble? Put my mother on display and not somehow catch my reaction?"

Sawyer inhaled. "Son of a bitch."

He took off, yelling for them to stay put as he headed for the nearest security station. He flashed his badge at the man standing in the glass room, yanking open the door when the guy pressed the release button. Sawyer stormed inside, searching the monitors until he found the hallway he needed.

He turned around, pointing at the screen. "I need all the video for that camera for the past several hours."

The man glanced at the monitor then back at Sawyer. "I don't understand. Your partner already collected the video tapes about five minutes ago."

"Partner? What partner?"

The guard shuffled restlessly on his feet. "Tall, dark hair. He had all the proper identification. I believe his name was Special Agent Davies."

Anger heated his face as he glanced back at the monitor. Mallory leaned against the wall, flanked by Cole, her gaze drifting from the floor to inside the open cell. Though the image wasn't zoomed in, he didn't need a close-up to recognise the pain in her expression.

He swore under his breath and removed a photo, holding it up to the guard. "Is this Agent Davies?"

The man crowded the image, tilting his head before nodding. "That's the guy. Like I said. He had the proper identification. Said he was part of the murder investigation." The man motioned to the adjoining hallway. "He went that way."

"How long would it take him to clear the grounds?"

The guard's eyes darted to the side as the man appeared to consider the question. "If he hurried, he'd be clear by now. He could use the service entrance."

Sawyer slammed his hand on the console, embracing the jolt of pain that skirted up his arm. "Have them check, anyway. And if he is still here, I want his ass, understood?"

"Yes, sir."

The guard picked up a phone and relayed the message as Sawyer trudged out and down the hallway. Cole met him at the edge of the cell, his face stern. Sawyer gave the man a shake of his head as he moved over to Mallory's side. He brushed a hand along her arm, silently cursing when she trembled beneath his touch.

She graced him with a sympathetic half-smile before turning and resting her back on the wall. "Let me guess. The tape's gone."

"Apparently my *partner* grabbed it several minutes ago."

She chuckled, though it seemed more like a release of tension than anything else. "Carter?"

He grimaced. "The guard said the guy matched Davies' description."

She rounded on him. "Matched his description? Don't bullshit me, Sawyer. Did you show the guy a picture or not?"

He sighed, thankful when Cole joined them. "He gave a positive ID to Davies' picture."

"Fuck! How the hell is this guy still alive? Am I honestly supposed to believe Carter switched the vials or gave him just enough to knock him out—that the doctor was in on it and that after several hours in the morgue, Carter wheeled him out and Davies walked away as if nothing had happened? God, this is like some bad horror movie, only it's not."

"I don't know. Maybe it isn't Davies, but just someone who looks like him. Hell, Mal, maybe that evil twin scenario isn't so far-fetched. At this point, I'd believe just about anything."

She met his gaze. "Evil twin? You're seriously falling back to an evil twin?"

He shrugged. "It's possible."

She twisted slightly, staring down the hallway before leaning against the wall again and meeting his stare. "Sorry. This isn't your fault."

"It's not yours, either."

She snorted, but didn't answer.

He took her hand. "Whoever this is—whether it really is Davies or Carter or some creep off the street—this is their doing. And nothing short of Biblical intervention could have changed what happened here today. I know that doesn't make you feel any better but, shit, darling. Please don't let this bastard beat you."

She gave his hand a squeeze. "Can we go now?"

He glanced at Cole then back to her. "Of course."

Cole waved at them. "I'll wait for Fisher. I'm sure he'll give me a lift back. You two should head home. I'll meet up with you later."

Sawyer paused. "You sure?"

"Absolutely. I want to make sure everything is taken care of properly."

Sawyer smiled his thanks. "We'll expect you at the house later."

Mallory waved off his suggestion. "Make it the pub. I need a drink." She whirled on Sawyer, shaking her finger at him. "And don't even think about lecturing me."

Sawyer shook his head. "I'll buy the first five rounds."

Cole tsked them. "Just don't get so drunk you can't drive home. I've seen what happens in the front of that Jeep. I don't want to be anywhere near that seat."

Sawyer smiled ever so slightly. Count on Cole to try and lighten the mood. "I'll keep that in mind." He palmed the small of Mallory's back as they headed out, giving the cell one last glance. Another victim and another stab at Mallory's sanity. He could only hope this one didn't bleed.

* * * *

Sawyer sat at the bar, silently watching as Mallory thumbed a glass of whisky, her attention seemingly focused on the deep brown liquid as it swirled around the edges, reflecting splashes of white from the overhead lights. She looked barren. Defeated. He hadn't left her side in hours, waiting for her to break down, but he suspected what she'd told Cole earlier had been the truth. She'd been mourning her mother for twenty years, and she just didn't have anything left to grieve over. Sure, she'd shed a few tears, but he could only guess that the pain had long ago faded into numbness, and not even death had managed to shake it.

He took another pull of his beer, glancing at the door to see if Cole had arrived yet. Mallory had insisted on stopping at the office and filling out the proper reports. Even Don had told her to go home, but she'd stubbornly stayed until there was nothing more to be done. Then they'd headed to the bar, where he'd expected her to drink herself to oblivion, but she'd only had two drinks, spending the rest of the time staring into the third.

He sighed and reached for her hand. "Why don't we just head home?"

She stopped swirling the liquor and looked at him. "I thought we were waiting for Cole?"

"The man owns a cell. I can call him and tell him to drive to the house, instead."

She pursed her lips up and down, as if unsure what to do before expelling a long breath. He pushed off the chair and moved behind her, gently laying his hands on her shoulders. She relaxed against him, allowing him to bear some of her weight.

He wrapped his arms around her shoulders and dropped a kiss on the top of her head. "It wasn't your fault."

She exhaled a shaky breath. "I should have been able to save her. It was the least I owed her."

"There was no way you could have known she'd be the next target."

"I should have guessed."

"Why, because she fit the profile?" Sawyer released her and spun her around on the stool. "Mal. This wasn't something either of us would have ever imagined. Your mother doesn't even get close to the type of women Davies went after. Even if you had suggested it, I would have shot you down because it was so outside the realm of the possible I never could have seen it coming." He paused, but decided not to hold back. "To be honest, I thought his next target would be you."

Her gaze clashed with his. "Me? But I don't fit the profile, either."

"You would have a couple of years ago. And I have a strange feeling you were on Davies' list, but we got lucky and caught him before he was able to do more than stab you."

"That doesn't make sense. If he wanted to kill me, why kill my mother?"

"Because she was an easy target. And because he knew it would hurt you." He raised his hand and cupped her jaw, tracing a line back with his finger. "Maybe this is payback for you besting him. For his failure. Or maybe he's just plain batshit crazy. I wish I had the answers, but I don't. All I know is that it'll be a cold fucking day in hell before he lays a finger on you."

Mallory's eyes softened and she reached up, drawing him down for a soul-searing kiss. He opened willingly as her tongue swept into his mouth, tangling with his. She swallowed his moan as he slid a hand behind her back, pulling her flush to his chest. Tiny buds poked at him, the hard peaks begging for his attention. He nipped at her neck when she released him, whispering his intentions when a raspy breath sounded behind him.

"You know, if you're trying to keep your relationship a secret, you're doing a lousy job."

Sawyer sighed and glanced over his shoulder, glaring at Cole as the man stood a few feet away, his one good arm crossed on his chest. Rain dotted his coat and it looked as if he'd been standing outside for a while.

Sawyer resisted the curse poised on his tongue and eased back, giving the room a quick scan. Several other agents were scattered around the bar and more than a few sets of eyes were focused their way. He thought about releasing his hold on Mallory, but decided against it.

He slid his fingers around her side, taking her hand in his. "I think we're past the secrecy part."

Cole chuckled. "Good, 'cause I think Fisher snapped a few shots before he left with Daniel…said something about winning the pool." He scraped back the stool beside Mallory, sinking into it with a weary breath. "Is it too late to join you for that drink?"

Mallory shook her head. "We were just about to make a toast."

"It looked more like you were just about to find a vacant wall, but whatever."

Mallory hit him in his good arm as she signalled for the bartender. The man brought over Cole's usual beer and moved on, helping another customer. Cole twisted off the cap then turned to look at them, the bottle gripped in his hand.

Mallory took a deep breath then held up her glass. "To Pamela Reeves and the night she saved my life."

Cole glanced at him over Mallory's shoulder as he raised his beer and took a long drink. Though he didn't say anything, Sawyer could see the concern in the man's eyes. He knew she'd wanted to say more — to add in the part where she hadn't reciprocated the favour — but the slump in her shoulders said it all. He tried to think of something comforting to say, when Mallory placed her glass on the counter.

She looked over at Cole. "So, are you going to tell us what Fisher had to say, or do we wait until Davies calls again to tell me personally?"

Cole set his beer down, giving Sawyer a hardened glance before swearing under his breath. "Now's not really the time, Mal. Take a break."

"Why, because that asshole's going to? He killed my mother to make a point. I'd like to make sure I don't miss what that point is."

"There wasn't much new, other than the picture of you on the sash."

She tilted her head. "And?"

Cole shrugged. "And what?"

"And what else? Don't shit me, Cole. You can't tell me Davies altered his entire MO just to put a picture of me on the damn sash. This goes much deeper than that. And if we want to finally catch the bastard, it might be best if we figure out his next step before it bites us in the ass."

Cole sighed and took another swig, downing half of what was left. "It's not what he left behind that's odd, it's what he omitted. For starters, there was no evidence of rape, though he probably wouldn't have had the time. There weren't any ligature marks on her ankles, either. We'll have to wait for the coroner to give a positive cause of death, but Fisher's pretty certain she bled out from the stab wound...wounds. There were several of them, actually. Most of them on her back."

Mallory glanced back at Sawyer, her brow furrowed. "Back? Since when the hell does Davies kill his victims by stabbing them? And why the back? He always struck from the front based on the evidence and Davies' testimony." She pounded one fist on the counter. "None of this makes sense."

"There's one other thing." Cole looked them both in the eyes. "There was a trace of foundation on the sash. Not enough for DNA, but it's the first time. I suppose there's a chance it belonged to your mother, but she wasn't wearing any makeup when they found her."

"She rarely wore it. I suppose it stemmed from not wanting any additional attention from my father. But I don't see her dolling herself up in prison." She looked away for a moment. "Wait. How many times was she stabbed?"

Cole snorted. "Sorry, Mal, I didn't count. I just heard Fisher mention it as something unusual, especially since the guard identified Davies at the scene. He thought it was odd the guy would alter his approach so much. To be honest, this one was a bit hard to swallow."

Mallory patted his hand. "Thanks. For staying."

"I figured it was the least I could do for you." He motioned to the bartender. "Want another?"

She shrugged.

Sawyer palmed her shoulder. "Maybe it's best if we head home. We can go over the details there if you want. Just do me a favour and hang with Cole while I use the men's room."

"I don't need a babysitter."

Cole huffed. "Good, 'cause I'm not wiping your ass if you have an accident."

Mallory sighed. "Fine. Go do your business. Cole's already offered to buy me another drink."

Sawyer ran a finger down her jaw as he gave her a smile. "I'll be right back."

Mallory watched Sawyer head for the hallway. She'd never seen him this protective before, not that she was really complaining. His concern was touching, and after everything that had happened, she could use a shoulder to lean on. Hell, she could use an entire body. She looked back at the counter as the bartender filled her glass. The scent of the rich brown whisky billowed around her, but it only made her stomach retch. She didn't want the alcohol. She wanted Sawyer. Wanted him holding her in their bed. Wanted him telling her it would all be all right, even if it was a lie. She closed her eyes, wondering when she'd turned so soft, when Cole's chuckle drew her attention.

She turned to him, drawing her brows together. "What the hell are you laughing about?"

He smiled. "You. Damn, Mal, you're so in love with him, you can't even see straight."

"I can't see straight because of the whisky."

"I've seen you down half a bottle and still kick some creep's ass. You've barely touched the stuff. Face it. This is all Sawyer."

"And if it is? Is that a problem?"

"Not as long as you two do it right this time."

Mallory resisted the smile tugging at her lips. "I didn't realise there was a wrong way to do it."

"Apparently, for you guys, anything involving the use of a bed is wrong."

"Very funny, Cole." She glanced at the hallway. "Shouldn't Sawyer be back by now?"

"He's probably kicking the walls to see if any are strong enough to withstand a quick round."

She sneered at him and slid to her feet. "Then I guess I'll go check. Save him the hassle of dragging me all the way back there."

Cole followed suit. "I'll tag along."

"Hoping to become that third after all?"

"Let's just say I don't want to get on Sawyer's bad side where you're concerned."

She gazed at the hallway again. "Shit. He told you not to let me out of your sight, didn't he?"

"He's just worried about you, as am I. This thing with Davies... It's gone way beyond a simple case, and neither of us are willing to put your safety on the line. So if you're going to pout, do it now, 'cause things aren't changing any time soon."

"Men. Did it ever occur to you that you're both in just as much danger?"

Cole winked at her. "We're your partners. That's just a given where you're concerned."

"I take it back. You can sleep at the foot of the bed instead of in the middle."

"I'm going to tell Sawyer you said that."

"Snitch."

"But I'm yours, honey. And apparently Sawyer's, too."

Mallory shook her head as she walked across the room and rounded the corner. The washrooms were down the hallway and around another bend. Already the sounds from the bar were dimmed, only the faint clanking of glasses echoing along the small corridor.

Cole grabbed her arm as she reached the halfway point. "Do you hear something?"

She tilted her head towards the corner. "Just a bunch of drunks singing—wait. It sounds like scuffling." She inhaled sharply. "Sawyer."

Cole held firm, unholstering his gun as he motioned towards the corner. She palmed her gun, darting to the inside of the turn. A flash reflected off the wall, followed by a grunt as something hit the floor. Hard.

Bile crested the back of her throat. God, she couldn't lose Sawyer. Not now. Not after finally getting him back. Cole met her gaze and counted to three, then stepped out. Mallory followed, sweeping the area with her gun. Sawyer was on the ground, his body spasming as another man darted for the rear door. Cole yelled, but the guy disappeared into the adjoining alleyway, nothing but a blur of black amidst the shadows.

Mallory beat Cole to Sawyer's side, checking his pulse while Cole holstered his weapon and did a quick body sweep.

"He's okay, Mal. That bastard hit him with a Taser...a few times. But it's nothing life-threatening."

Mallory dropped to her knees, cradling Sawyer's head. "Fuck. How long were they fighting?"

Cole lifted Sawyer's shirt, exposing a string of marks along his ribs. "Several minutes judging on the wounds. Looks like the impact sites were across his ribs. Not as many nerves or muscles to pass along the signal. Probably what allowed him to fight back, though it must have hurt like hell. Most likely saved his life, though."

She clenched her jaw, fighting back angry tears. This was it. The point of no return. Either they caught the bastard or he won. She glanced at the door. It'd only been a minute. He wouldn't have that far of a lead, especially if this was part of some larger plan like she suspected. A hand grabbed her arm and she looked down.

Sawyer stared up at her, his face distorted with pain. "Don't...eve...thi...it."

His words were garbled, but she got the gist of it.

She bent closer. "Who attacked you?"

He closed his eyes as if talking took more energy than he possessed. "Dav...vies."

She patted his hand, hoping he'd understand. "This ends tonight." She shook her head when he tried to lever himself upright. "We both know he's planning much more than abducting you. And now that you've ruined it, he'll be off kilter. This is the first time things haven't gone as planned for him. The first time he's not in control. We need to capitalise on that." She pulled out her phone and held it up. "You can track me with any one of those GPS apps. I'll turn them all on and set my phone to vibrate. Just be there when I need you. Both of you."

She pushed up when Cole stepped in front of her.

He shook his head. "This is crazy, especially if you think I'm going to let you go alone."

"I won't be alone, at least not for long. Just let me confront him. That's what he wants. Sawyer was right. Davies wanted me to be his last victim. If we show up together, he'll just disappear again and we'll be left with nothing more than another dead body."

"What makes you think he's got another girl?"

"Because he always had a backup plan."

Cole scrubbed his hand down his face. "You don't even know where he is. Shit, Mal, he's got minutes on you."

"He doesn't want to lose me, Cole. Trust me." She reached for his hand. "I'm counting on you."

She blew Sawyer a kiss, mouthing for him to be there then ran for the door.

Chapter Thirteen

Rain pelted against Mallory's face, stinging her skin as she ran down the alley, stopping at the rear street. Passing lights illuminated the drops, casting rainbow-coloured streaks in the puddles lacing the road. She searched each direction, looking for any hint of movement, anything remotely out of place that would prove she was right and that the bastard wanted her to follow him. Signs creaked as the wind gusted down the narrow road, but everything seemed quiet.

"Fuck!"

She headed for a nearby alleyway, guessing that Davies wouldn't stick to the main roads, and ducked down the entrance, squinting to see through the shadows. A garbage can clattered near the rear, followed by the muffled sound of footsteps.

She cursed. Why did it always come back to alleyways?

Mallory crept down the corridor, sticking to the sides, encasing herself in the dark. Distant thunder rumbled across the sky, adding a slight vibration to the air. She took it slow, knowing she had time. If it was Davies ahead, then she'd been right, and the bastard had grander plans than striking at Sawyer. The thought sent a rush of ice water through her veins. If Sawyer hadn't fought back, if he wasn't as strong as a damn ox, Davies might have dragged him off.

She shook the images from her mind. Sawyer had just been the bait. Something to get her on Davies' turf. She was his real target and even without Sawyer as leverage, Mallory knew the man would have alternate arrangements. Something or someone else to bargain with. It didn't matter what or who, it only mattered that more than just her life would be on the line.

She reached the end of the alley and stopped, listening for more movement. Something crashed off to her left. She peeked down the small cross street, clearing the other side before starting down, still keeping to the edges. Rain dripped down her forehead, chilling her skin as she followed the road, coming to another street. This one was larger than the others, with small houses occupying the other side. She studied the area when something twigged. She'd been here before, a few years back. They'd raided a house Carter had insisted belonged to Davies, but it'd been a bust.

More pieces fell into place and she turned left again, heading for the same location. This wasn't a coincidence. This was fate on a grandiose scale. And she knew exactly where to go.

The road twisted a few times, crossing more streets, before she reached her destination. A small brown house set back from the road called like a beacon in the night, the glow of a single light the only clue that she was right. She opened the gate, not even winching when the damn thing squeaked, and walked up to the porch. The second step groaned and creaked, but she ignored it. He already knew she was coming.

She stopped at the threshold, glancing down at the handle. The door stood slightly ajar, dissolving any thoughts that she was wrong or that this house belonged to someone else. She gave the door a shove, clearing the room as it swung open, allowing the area beyond to ghost into view. A long hallway led to the rear of the house, with a few doorways branching off to her right. She entered slowly, checking behind her as she moved along the hallway, making her way towards the back. She'd almost reached the kitchen when a noise rose from behind one of the doors.

Mallory stared at the door, knowing what she had to do, but hating every second of it. This was it. There was no going back once she opened the door. She reached for her pocket, ensuring her phone was still there. She had no idea where the boys were, but she had to believe they wouldn't let her down.

She took a deep breath then palmed the handle, slowly opening the door. The hinges screeched as it swung inward, the sound raising the hairs along the nape of her neck. She held her Glock out in front of her, aiming at the man's head as it appeared at the rear of the room, largely hidden behind the body of a young woman. The silver sheen of a blade gleamed in the dull light as it hovered at the woman's throat, the tip drawing a drop of bright red blood from her skin. The girl's eyes widened as she whimpered, the soft moans muffled by a piece of duct tape placed across her mouth. Blood oozed from several wounds, but nothing that appeared deep enough to kill her.

The man smiled. "Ah, Special Agent Reeves. Right on time. How nice of you to accept my invitation."

Mallory did a quick scan of the floor in front of her before stepping inside. Her gaze locked on his. God, he looked exactly the same—slicked-back hair above bulging eyes. The angles of his face were hard and pronounced, making him look every inch the killer he was.

She forced down a swallow. "It was more of a demand than a request."

He laughed. "Either way, it was your choice to come here. Which reminds me. I'm impressed. I wasn't sure you'd remember this place."

"You're not an easy man to forget."

He raised an eyebrow. "Now, Agent Reeves, that almost sounds like admiration."

"It's more revulsion than anything else, but it doesn't change the fact that you're a hard man to track down. Though it helps when you're masquerading to be someone you aren't."

His smile dimmed slightly. "Are you suggesting I'm not who I claim to be? That I'm not the person responsible for all those deaths? Are you admitting you tried to kill an innocent man?"

"Oh, you're a killer. In fact, you're a fucking psychopath. You just aren't John Davies."

The smile vanished. "And who am I then?"

"The same man you've always been...Derek Carter."

He stared at her, his fingers tightening on the knife. More blood welled up from the wound, mocking her. Right or wrong, she needed to alter the nature of the game before nothing she did had any positive outcomes.

A cruel sneer finally captured his lips as he took a calculated step to his left. "I'm disappointed, Agent Reeves. I thought you knew me better than that, or did your mother's death affect you to the point you don't even recognise the man who has so clearly beaten you?"

"Whether you've beaten me or not doesn't change the fact that you're not John Davies." She chuckled. "Perhaps they should call me Daphne after all, because in the end, this monster turned out to be nothing more than a man in a mask, albeit a very convincing one. I'm assuming that masterpiece is latex. Form-fitting and every bit a testament to Hollywood. Must have cost you a small fortune. And I have to say, the voice was a nice touch. Who knew you had so many hidden talents."

He growled in defiance, jerking the girl back in his arms. The knife slipped, drawing a smile cut along her skin. She screamed behind the tape, the sound nothing more than a muted sigh as blood dripped from the wound and down her chest.

He glared at Mallory, his lips pulled back to expose a row of crooked teeth, identical to the ones Davies had flashed her at the execution. "You're guessing."

"Am I? No rape or ligature marks on my mother. Multiple stab wounds. Davies never would have deviated from his MO like that. He was too perfect, too obsessed. His pleasure came from the details...from proving, over and over, that he was in control. Her death didn't have any of that. It was simply a man making a statement. And I heard you. Besides, Davies always called me Mallory, not Agent Reeves. He liked the morbid intimacy of it."

"So you're basing your hypothesis on one altered death and a name? Not very professional of you...*Mallory*."

"But right, just the same." She inched to the left. "We know about the tampered evidence in the Thomas case. I'm starting to think it wasn't a coincidence that his lawyer discovered the planted blood samples. Were you hoping to discredit our investigation as well? Set Davies free with the same claim?" She paused but he remained silent. "Or maybe it was all a ploy to torment the man. Maybe you never planned on saving his life."

"There's nothing to save. I'm standing right in front of you."

"There were traces of latex in the wounds. We'd figured it was surgical gloves, but we were wrong. The victims must have scratched bits of your mask. There was also a smudge of foundation on my mother's sash, but she wasn't the one wearing the makeup...it was you." She shook her head. "I have to hand it to you, Carter. You look just like the son of a bitch. Same piercing eyes. Hell, you're even the same body build. But as good as you are, I can tell the difference."

He smiled. "Should I take that as a compliment? Have you been studying me?"

"It's always wise to study one's enemies."

"You tell a nice story, but in the end, you're still just guessing. Did it occur to you that I left those clues behind on purpose?"

"I saw the video tape of the execution. You counted on everything except a reflection on the glass." She nodded at him. "You had me convinced. The alleyway, the old house, the phone call. Stealing Davies' body out from under our noses at the morgue, not to mention killing the doctor from the execution — that was a touch of brilliance. The final few pieces you needed to cast doubt on Davies' death. I honestly believed you'd somehow brought the bastard back from Hell. But you screwed up when you killed my mother in exactly the same fashion she murdered my father. This isn't about Davies or the women he killed. It's about me. You simply used the one man who'd gotten to me to do it."

He held her stare before his mouth curled into a wide smile. "Touché. I have to hand it to you. You're good. Better than good, actually." He sighed, raising one hand to tear at his face. Chunks of rubbery skin fell to the ground, revealing the left side of Carter's face as his lips twisted into a sadistic grin. "The glass. What were the chances of that? Thought I'd stayed off to the side enough to prevent any reflections, but you can't account for every angle of every camera. Technology. It really is a motherfucker."

"Where's Davies' body?"

"Let's just say I've got it on ice, just in case."

She held her ground, purposely not staring at the pieces of Davies' artificial flesh littering the floor. "Why don't you let the woman go? Then you and I can have a chat...just the two of us."

He laughed. "Do you honestly take me for a fool? No, this is going to end the way it should have two years ago. The perfect finish to my reign of terror."

His words hit her hard and she tried not to flinch. God, what had she missed?

"Didn't see that one coming, did you? Thought I'd merely picked up where Davies had left off? That he'd gotten inside my head and sent me off the proverbial deep end? Sorry to disappoint you, but it appears there were still a few loose ends you hadn't tied up just yet. Connections you never made." His eyes lit up. "Oh, my dear, Mallory. The part I enjoyed the most was watching all of you puzzle it out. Unearthing Davies was always part of my plan. I'm afraid the man was fucking crazy. Completely off the chart. But we shared a common vision—one that allowed me to control his desires, shall we say."

Mallory tried to swallow past the lump in her throat. "Did you frame Davies the way you framed Thomas, you son of a bitch?"

"Now don't go jumping to conclusions. I assure you. Davies was as sick as you thought he was. He just wasn't the brains behind the operation. He was a man of action. Liked to get his hands dirty. Liked the way the blood looked and tasted. He was more than eager to do my bidding and play the part of the main character. There was just one problem. The man couldn't think past his own demons. Couldn't deviate from a single step. He was meticulous to a fault. It was only a matter of time before he got caught."

"So why didn't the crazy bastard turn you in? Why take the fall if you were his partner?"

"Because he trusted me. I was his mentor of sorts, and I assured him we'd be the ones to finally bring the FBI to its knees. He had a problem with authority."

More pieces clicked into place as she shuffled forward, halting when he glared at her.

She nodded at him. "You never planned to save him, did you? You were there to ensure he died."

"I hate loose ends. As you can see for yourself, they have a way of coming back and, how did you put it, 'biting you in the ass'."

"You shot Cole and attacked Sawyer. Looks like you're getting sloppy."

"Am I? Or was it a conscious decision *not* to kill them."

Dread churned in her stomach, making it burn. "You want them to suffer."

"Couldn't have your knights in shining armour riding to the rescue. Nasty things those

Tasers…almost as debilitating as a bullet wound. I'm betting Sawyer won't be able to move properly for another hour or so, seeing as I hit him half a dozen times. He did surprise me, though. I didn't think he'd be so hard to take down. He's stronger than I gave him credit." He winked at her. "And here I thought you were the one with the stamina after that lovely display in the Jeep. Now I see where your mother got her lusty ways from."

"My mother? Lusty? And you said Davies was the crazy one. I'm afraid you've got the facts wrong."

"Or maybe you didn't know her all that well. After all, she never really wanted you, did she?"

It wasn't a question and Mallory wasn't going to grace him with an answer. "Ancient history."

"Ah, but isn't history supposed to teach us about the future?" He cocked his head to the side. "You really did spend all your time hiding from your father. Shame. I'm told your mother put on quite the show between the sheets."

"What my mother did was stay with a man who beat her."

"Maybe she enjoyed it."

He held up his hand, sliding the knife a bit farther along the woman's neck, repositioning the tip as she jerked in his arms.

"I know what you're thinking, but even if you manage to kill me, the woman will still die. No matter how I fall, the knife will cut her artery, and we both know what happens next."

"I thought you wanted me to be your final victim?"

"All in good time." He nodded at a chair off to her right. "Sit."

She hesitated. He tsked and shoved the tip deeper. The woman made a gurgling noise as she slumped against him.

Mallory moved over to the seat. "Easy, Carter."

"Then don't fuck with me." He eased his grip as she slid into the chair. "Better."

"So why should I care if my mother enjoyed sex?"

"Because your father wasn't the only one she was having it with." He smiled. "You see, you and I aren't that different. We both had fathers we'd rather forget. My father was a cop, but not just any cop. He was a beat cop in one of the toughest districts in the city. Do you know what that meant? It meant he didn't have to abide by the rules. It meant that when he beat his wife and his kid, his friends looked the other way. It's all part of their stupid code—watching out for each other. Hiding the truth for each other. Brothers in arms and all that bullshit. It went on for years until one day, she didn't come home, and I was all that stood between him and his drunken rages. Then he found your mother and things got better. He stopped drinking and hitting, and for a moment—one precious fucking moment—he was nearly human. That all changed the night she decided to get rid of your father, and it all started again." He sneered at her. "If you hadn't been there, she wouldn't have gone to jail, and I wouldn't have had to suffer at the hands of that bastard. Do you have any idea what he did to me?"

"I can imagine."

"No! I don't think you can." His voice echoed off the walls as he shuffled to the other wall. "You had someone to save you. I was alone. Abandoned by the women who should have been the ones to take his abuse—to spare me the agony of being raped by that bastard. All those years." His voice cracked and he chuckled. "And it all started with you."

"So why kill those other women?"

He smiled. "I think you know why."

"What makes you think you can stop once I'm dead?"

"You have a point, but that's just a chance I'll have to take." He straightened. "Now, you have a choice to make. Either I kill this innocent girl, or you agree to take her place."

"And if I don't choose to save her?"

"You will. You're not like me and besides, you wouldn't want Don's niece to pay for your mistakes." He nodded. "She really should watch the kind of men she gets into cars with. Never can tell if they're what they say they are."

"Shit." She stood. "Let her go, and I'll take her place."

"Again, I'm not an idiot. You toss away that lovely Glock and sit back down on the chair, facing the door, and we'll see how generous I'm feeling."

"No way, Carter. I'm not an idiot, either." She motioned towards the doorway. "Why don't we take this into the kitchen? You can let her go out the back door while I sit at the table."

His gaze darted to the hallway. "Or I can just kill her now."

"Kill your only leverage? You said you weren't crazy."

"Fair enough. You first."

Mallory moved towards the door, never taking her eyes off Carter. He followed, keeping the girl positioned in front of him, never giving her a clear shot. She shifted right once she reached the hallway, walking towards the end of the house. Shadows played along the walls, making weird patterns across the floor. She sidestepped into the kitchen and headed for the table.

"That's far enough, Mallory." Carter shuffled in behind her, stopping between her and the back door. "Unlock the door then sit down."

She nodded, twisting the lock before sliding into the seat closest to her. The girl stumbled along with Carter, her pale skin a sharp contrast to the oppressive darkness.

"Put your gun on the table and weave your hands together behind your head."

She did as he asked, clasping her fingers together as he inched his way to the door. He scanned the area, then opened the door and pushed the girl out, closing it behind him. Mallory heard the girl trip her way down the stairs before an eerie silence filled the room.

Carter sighed as he pointed a Beretta at her. "You knew I had a gun, didn't you."

"I would have." She drew a quick breath. "But you're not going to use it. Not on me. You see, I don't think Davies was the only one who got pleasure from the details. You'll want this to be as accurate as possible to that night. That means you need me back in the bedroom."

"Clever. And correct. But know this. I want you dead more than I want the perfect scene, so don't think I won't shoot you in the back if you so much as twitch."

She rose from the chair, slowly making her way towards the bedroom again. She kept her back to the hallway, electing to watch every step Carter made. Her phone vibrated in her pocket, but she ignored it, turning into the room as she crested the doorway. Carter stepped in behind her and closed the door.

He motioned to the small bed in the far left corner. "Not quite the setup you had, but I like it. It's more reminiscent of my room." He smiled. "Unfortunate your partners couldn't join you, but they'll be seeing you soon. Sit on the bed."

She shuffled over, resting her hip on the edge of the bed. "This isn't going to stop those demons in your head. You know that. Killing me...it'll only make them louder. Believe me. I've heard them before."

"But that's where we're different. You hide from them while I...I embrace them."

"Believe what you want, but you're hiding, too." She took a deep breath, waiting for the numbing fear to course through her veins as memories of that night resurfaced. But instead she felt a sense of peace. Everything slowed around her and she relaxed. "This won't turn out the way you intend. Nothing good will come from this."

"I'm only finishing what we started. You and me — this case. You see, Davies was only supposed to gain your attention that night. Keep you busy while I got a chance to knock you out. But the damn fool got scared when you interrupted him and stabbed you instead. Pity he isn't here to see our work come to fruition."

"This isn't going to end the way you've envisioned."

"Is that so? I've seen you fight, but even you can't outmanoeuvre a bullet. And on the off chance Sawyer and Cole do manage to track you down, I'll know the second they get close. I'm afraid it'll be too late."

"What makes you so sure?"

"Do you honestly think I didn't prepare for your company?"

She allowed the smile tugging at her mouth to lift the edges. "I have no doubt you did, but there's just one problem with your theory. What if they're already inside?"

Surprise widened his eyes and Mallory moved, diving off the bed as Sawyer popped out from behind it, hitting Carter in the shoulder with a single round. The man reeled backwards only to jerk forward as Cole crashed through the door, his shot hitting the creep square in the torso. Blood arced up the walls and across the ceiling as the man crumpled on the floor, his gun skipping across the old wood.

Mallory drew in a much-needed breath, staring up at Sawyer as he stumbled out from behind the bed, nearly tripping over his feet. He braced his weight on the wall as he glared down at her.

"Of all the dumbass stunts to pull—"

She jumped up and silenced him with a kiss, her arms reaching around to encircle her neck. He leant back, bridging both their weight as he returned the kiss, finally pulling back. His expression softened slightly, but she knew he was far from happy.

She glanced over at Carter, watching as Cole checked for a pulse. He shook his head, closing the man's eyes as he pushed to his feet.

She eased away from Sawyer, accepting the gun Cole handed her. "Before you both start, you know it was the right thing to do. He would have kept killing if I hadn't confronted him."

Sawyer crossed his arms on his chest. "Right or wrong, you're just damn lucky one of those bloody apps worked. The first one kept telling us you were at the fucking airport."

"That's just the starting point, Einstein. From the last time you used it." She laughed. "You really need to learn how to use that thing."

"I know how to use my *thing* just fine. It's you I can't handle." He held out his hand, pulling her against his chest. "Just don't scare me like that again. Ever."

"Deal." She pushed away. "Damn. Don's niece. He shoved her out the back door."

"She's fine. Well, alive. I darted back out when I heard him close the door and sent her to the truck. Ambulance is already on the way." Cole shook his head. "You do know that's not Don's niece, right? Not unless she's looking really grown-up for a twelve-year-old."

Mallory drew her brows together. "Say again? I know there's a photo on Don's desk of a girl about her age and colouring."

"That photo came with the damn frame, Sherlock. You know how bad Don is about that kind of stuff. Promised his wife he'd change it years ago. Guess he hasn't had time yet." He nodded at the door. "Now, if you two think you can handle one dead creep, I'll go back out and wait with her. Niece or not, she's pretty freaked out."

Mallory nodded, stepping over to Carter's lifeless body.

Sawyer moved in behind her, brushing his chest against her back. "You okay?"

She shrugged. "He did all of this—killed all those women—just to get to me."

"He killed all of those women because he enjoyed it, plain and simple. The guy was a nut job. It's just too bad we didn't discover that until now." He gave her a nudge. "Come on. Let's get out of here. I've had enough of Davies and Carter for one day." He took a step then stopped. "Where is Davies?"

Mallory gave his shoulder a pat. "You don't want to know."

Sawyer groaned as they headed out the door. "Damn, Carter did something disgusting, didn't he? Like put him in a rocking chair in a room somewhere."

"That was Norman Bates. I think Davies is in the freezer."

"I thought you weren't going to tell me?"

"I changed my mind seeing as you lied to me." She stopped and turned into him. "You said you'd be right back."

He released a ragged breath. "I didn't see the creep until he hit me with the damn Taser."

"You scared me."

"Good. Now you know what it's like to be your partner."

She shook a finger at him. "Don't do it again, or—"

"Or what, darling?"

"Or I might have to do something drastic."

"Such as…"

"I don't know. Something rash, like…like asking you to marry me."

Sawyer grabbed her shoulders when she went to turn around, spinning her back to face him. "What did you just say?"

She closed the scant distance between them, pressing her body against his. "I said, will you marry me?"

Emotions crossed his face, flashing in and out of his eyes before one side of his mouth lifted into a smile. "I'm pretty sure you're a couple of years late on that particular question."

"Never hurts to be sure."

"Are you?" He took a deep breath. "Sure?"

She smiled and slipped her hands around the back of her neck as she unclipped her necklace and laid it across one palm. Something sparkled in the light as she removed the ring he'd given her and refastened her chain. She held his gaze as she pushed it on her finger, twisting it until the diamond cast speckled dots along the wall. "Pretty damn sure."

Sawyer stared at her, then brushed his finger across the surface. "When the hell did you put that on there? I swear I haven't seen it, and darling, I've seen a lot of you, lately."

"This morning. After everything that happened last night, it just didn't feel right not to have it close to me." She took a fortifying breath. "Unless you'd rather I didn't. Wear it, that is."

"Are you fucking serious?" He grabbed his wallet and opened the small zippered pouch, removing a matching band. "I only took this off to come here. I didn't want to push you into anything you weren't ready for."

"So is that a yes?"

He winked and yanked her into his chest. "I'll let you know in a couple more years."

Chapter Fourteen

Sawyer sat on the edge of the bed, staring down at his feet. Pain radiated through his body and he wondered how the hell he was going to get his socks off. A bemused laugh sounded off to his right before a pair of bare feet entered his line of sight. He smiled as Mallory knelt beside him, looking up at him with an easy love that spiked his heart rate.

"Contemplating your place in the universe?"

"Close. I was thinking how the hell I was going to get my socks off."

"That was close."

She reached for his feet, the diamond in her ring glinting in the light. The sight quickened his breath and he remembered the look in her eyes when she'd asked him to marry her. A tremble skirted down his spine as she removed his socks then climbed on the bed, motioning him to swing his legs up. He clenched his jaw then levered back, grunting as the movement irritated the shallow wounds on his ribs.

Mallory pursed her lips. "Are you sure you don't need to go to the hospital?"

He gave her a sly smile as he glanced at the clock on the side table. "Less than four hours since you asked me to marry you and already you're trying to get rid of me. That doesn't bode well."

She huffed and smacked his leg. "You're an ass."

"But I'm your ass, darling."

"Lucky me." She poked his leg. "Lift up and I'll take off your jeans."

He winked at her. "Shouldn't you disarm me, first?"

She leaned in, hovering her face inches from his. "I'm pretty sure I can handle whatever's inside, *baby*."

He chuckled and lifted his hips, panting through the pain as she slipped the zipper free and removed his pants, tossing them to the floor. Her gaze swept up his body, pausing at the bruises lining his ribs.

A frown tugged at her luscious mouth, making her full lips protrude ever so slightly. "Good God. Have you seen what that bastard did to you?"

He shook his head, reaching forward to cup her chin in his hand as he caressed her jaw with his thumb. "Nope. I've got something far better to look at."

Her gaze flew to his, the soft lines around her eyes crinkling as a genuine smile curled her lips. "Were you always this charming?"

"Probably not."

"I didn't think so." She glanced down his body again, this time swiping her tongue across her lower lip as her gaze paused at his groin. "I was thinking...since sex is obviously out of the question—"

"Who said sex was out of the question?"

"Are you serious? You couldn't even remove your socks."

"I don't have to bend over to have you ride me."

She tilted her head as she sighed. "And the pain in your ribs? I'm fairly certain any kind of movement, no matter how pleasurable, will be too much for them."

"Then you'll have to go slowly."

"Or…" She placed a finger over his mouth, silencing him. "I could simply give you the best blowjob in the history of blowjobs and call it a night."

He grabbed her as she started to move back. "If you think, after everything that's happened today, I'll be content without returning the favour, you're crazier than I thought."

Her eyes held his as she straddled his thighs. "You can make it up to me in the morning if you're any better."

"Mal—"

"Would you just shut up and let your wife give you a blowjob?"

The word sucked out his breath and he sat there, back braced against the headboard, his hands ready to grab her shoulders, staring at her. Doubts he hadn't realised he still harboured faded away, leaving only love to fill the empty space.

He closed his eyes against a rush of emotion, wondering what he'd done to deserve her, when her lips brushed his. He forced his eyelids apart, instantly surrounded by a brilliant blue.

"I love you, Sawyer. I'm sorry it took me so long to realise that it wasn't you or getting married that I was afraid of. It was just the distorted memories of a ten-year-old girl, who'd spent her life hiding under the bed."

He traced a finger along her cheek. "She didn't hide. She survived."

"Either way, I don't need to hide when I have you. You're all the strength I need." Her lips quirked as she backed away. "Now be a good boy and let me perform my wifely duties."

"Now this, I could get used to." He winked at her. "Does this mean you'll start cooking me dinner?"

She chuckled. "You do know I'm about to put your cock in my mouth, right? I'd lay off the chauvinist remarks until after you come."

"Point taken. But I'm still going to recipro... Damn."

His words rasped into a groan as Mallory bent over him and wrapped her lips around his shaft, taking it deep to the back of her throat. Wet heat engulfed his skin, making the pain in his ribs a distant memory. He reached for her hair, holding it back so he could watch her move along his length. Study the way her lips stretched to accommodate his width or how the pink of her flesh contrasted with the pale white of his.

Fire tingled along his spine, threatening to unhinge him with a single pass of her mouth. He clenched his jaw, trying not to concentrate on the slow press of her tongue along the thick ridge or how she hummed in delight, sending small vibrations up his shaft.

"God. Darling. You're too good at this."

She glanced up at him—blue pools beneath black lashes. There were no doubts, no hidden hesitation in her eyes, only love, and raging desire.

The edges of her mouth tightened and he knew she was smiling at him.

He rolled his head back against the bed, acutely aware of every inch of her mouth on his cock. The way she hollowed her cheeks, creating pressure along the length of his shaft, or how her fingers caressed his sac, gently squeezing each side until he thought his head would explode. She was more than just his partner. She was the other half of his soul.

Mallory eased back, licking the tip before looking up at him. "Tell me. Do you want to come in my mouth, or inside me?"

A growl resonated through the air before he realised he'd made a sound. He grabbed her thin shirt and tugged her to him, answering her with a possessive sweep of his tongue in her mouth. She returned the kiss, tangling her tongue with his as she positioned herself above him, sliding the head of his cock through her drenched folds.

"Fuck. Mal."

He panted in an effort to breathe as she nipped at his neck, expertly aligning her sex up with his crown. Hot arousal covered his skin and it was all he could do not to empty his load all over her pussy.

"I'm far too gone for you to tease me, so I suggest you don't push it any farther."

"Or what? You'll come?" She chuckled. "Just close your eyes, and let me love you."

Her choice of words rippled heat out from his core in an ever-increasing wave. He palmed her hips, feeling every twitch of her muscles as she lowered her weight and sheathed him completely inside her. Contractions assaulted her cock as she levered back up, pausing at the top before lowering again, brushing her cream across his skin as she buried him deep inside again.

He grabbed her shirt, ripping it off before pulling her close and savouring every inch of skin on skin contact. This was how he wanted her. Writhing in his arms, so full of him she could barely breathe. She arched, throwing her head back as she quickened her pace, more flutters of need skittering along his shaft.

"Come for me."

Her eyes flew open and her gaze locked on his before her mouth opened in a soundless scream, her channel closing around his invasion. The increased pressure snapped his control and he thrust up, hilting himself inside as she convulsed through her release, a wash of hot cream coating his flesh. He grunted her name, pressing his head back as his cock jerked, emptying inside her. He held on, watching an array of coloured dots dance across the blackness before the fire dimmed, leaving him with a warm glow burning in his gut.

Mallory collapsed against him, her skin soft and warm on his. He wrapped his arms around her, drinking in the flowery scent of her soap and the musky aroma of their lovemaking. It was a combination he'd never grow tired of.

A gentle breath tickled his neck as she eased back, those brilliant eyes staring into his. She glanced down the bed, sighing in mock disgust.

"This wasn't exactly what I promised to give you." She looked up at him. "I suppose I owe you one."

"You can pay your debt off in the morning, right after I lick you into an orgasm."

"Mmm. I think I could get used to this wife thing. Does this mean you'll kill spiders for me?"

"I don't recall that being in the vows, but I'll consider it." He stopped. "Wait. You don't even remember those vows. Hell, you don't even remember saying *I do*."

She silenced him with a kiss, dropping another on his nose as she pulled away. "I remember wishing I'd never sent you away, which is far more important. I don't need a piece of paper to pledge my love. You already have it. But if you want, we can do it again...skip down to city hall, have Cole and his flavour of the month meet us there. I promise not to throw a fit this time."

Sawyer shook his head, reclaiming the lost inches between them. "Maybe later. I'd rather jump straight to the honeymoon phase."

"We'll have to come clean at work."

"Wouldn't want to keep Fisher from winning the pool." He drew her face to his. "I love you, Mallory Reeves."

"Kent. Special Agent Mallory Kent."

* * * *

"Sawyer. Mallory. Cole. My office. Now."

Mallory looked up from her report as Don's voice bellowed across the room. They'd spent the past couple of days immersed in paperwork and were finally ready to close the case. Don hadn't said a word, but she knew it was only a matter of time before he confronted them about their relationship—one they hadn't done a good job of hiding since their kiss in the bar the other night.

She sighed and stood, glancing over at Cole. The man smiled at her and she immediately wanted to smack the smug grin off his face. He'd been irritating as hell since he'd spied the rings on their fingers and she could only guess he'd been far from subtle where Don was concerned.

Cole stepped beside her. "Now I wonder why he wants all three of us in there?"

Mallory hit him across his good shoulder. "Probably because you said something you shouldn't have."

"I didn't say shit."

"You always say that, yet he always seems to know everything." She looked back at Sawyer. "Well, it was only a matter of time."

She walked forward, stepping through Don's open door. Three seats were lined up in front of his desk. She cringed. That was never a good sign.

Don motioned to the chairs. "Sit."

She headed for the far chair, but Cole beat her to it, smiling when she was forced to take the middle one. God, the arrangement made them appear every bit the freaky threesome some agents swore they were, and she groaned inwardly when Don closed the door before taking his place behind his desk again.

He cleared his throat as he picked up a stack of papers. "I've been going over the reports on the Davies-Carter case and I have to say…you three did a damn good job, despite the fact you used some highly unorthodox means of getting said job done." He mumbled something under his breath as he pushed to his feet. "Jesus, Mallory. I thought having another member on your team would help temper that reckless streak, but I see even Sawyer has trouble keeping you grounded." He held up a hand when Sawyer opened his mouth. "No blame intended, just stating a fact." He placed the reports back on his desk. "I will say one thing. You saved the Bureau a rather embarrassing lawsuit and gave more than a few families the closure they needed. While I don't always approve of your tactics, I can't argue with the results."

Mallory looked at the men, unsure what to say. It didn't feel as if Don was finished, and somehow thanking him at this point felt wrong.

Don took their silence as permission to continue. He picked up another envelope as he turned to her and Sawyer. "Now, speaking of bare asses…" He tossed the offering down in front of them. "Is there something the two of you want to tell me?"

Sawyer glanced at the envelope before meeting Don's gaze. "I think the photos are fairly self-explanatory, sir."

Don scrubbed a hand down his face. "They're definitely explicit, I'll grant you that. As for explanatory, all they really tell me is that you two are far more flexible than most people."

Mallory sighed, knowing there was no point dragging the conversation out further. They'd already discussed the possible outcomes and had agreed to make whatever changes were needed.

She held up her hand, drawing Don's attention. "What Sawyer means is, I think it's obvious by the photos that we're involved. Intimately involved."

Don snorted. "I got that. What I want to know is how involved are you?" He reached down and picked up another piece of paper. "The reason I ask is because I just got a transfer request from Albuquerque today with a notice from Washington stating that I'd be a fool not to ask Sawyer to rejoin our team. I couldn't help but notice you're both wearing matching jewellery, though these days that tends to be a passing fad. What I need to know is if he'll be staying or jumping ship again in a few months."

"He'll be staying."

"For how long?"

Sawyer patted her arm, indicating he'd answer this one. "Permanently, if I have anything to say in the matter."

Don scoffed and looked at her. "Does he have anything to say in the matter, Agent Reeves?"

"He definitely does, sir."

"And you're sure of this because…"

She smiled. "Because if we didn't divorce each other in the two years we were apart, I highly doubt we'll do it now that we're back together. I'm one of those people that believes in the whole 'til death thing."

Don's eyes widened in surprise before he regained his composure, sinking into his chair. "'Til death, huh?" He laughed, nodding at Sawyer. "I'd be very careful if I were you. That sounds more like a promise than a statement."

Sawyer gave her a stunning smile. "I'm having Kevlar pyjamas made, just in case."

Don shook his head, leaning his chair back. "Well, that changes things." He tossed the transfer paper on top of the pile on his desk. "Guess that means I'll be granting the transfer. It also means that Fisher won the damn pool. That man's going to be impossible to work with for the next few weeks." He reached for his mug and took a long drink before standing and moving over to the door. He opened it then turned back to face them. "Very well. I suggest you three finalise any last reports and get started on a new case. There's got to be a backlist by now. And again. Good work."

Mallory looked at Sawyer then at Don. "That's it?"

Don shrugged. "Did I forget something, other than asking you if you want to go by Reeves or Kent now?"

"Just the part where you yell and shuffle one of us off to some godforsaken department nobody wants to work in. And I was thinking I'd change it to Kent."

"Noted. And that'd be Fisher's department and neither of you are qualified as forensic technicians."

She raised one brow. "So we're staying together? All three of us?"

Don motioned to Cole. "You have a problem working with Bonnie and Clyde?"

Cole smiled. "Not as long as I don't have to drive the Jeep."

Don hid all but a hint of a smile. "I'd say that's fair. Anything else?"

She shook her head as she stood. "I guess that covers it."

Don sighed. "Look. Mallory. As long as the two of you remain field agents, the Bureau doesn't have any issues with you working together. If your status should change in the future, we might have to reassess, but until then, just try to stay clear of the paparazzi and don't make Cole drive the damn Jeep."

"Understood." She glanced over at Cole as they headed back to their desks. "But if you don't have to drive the Jeep, I shouldn't have to ride in the backseat of your truck. Talk about a Petri dish."

She dodged the wad of paper Cole tossed at her as he took his seat.

He nodded at them. "So if you guys are Bonnie and Clyde, who the hell am I?"

She shrugged. "You kind of have a Flo Rida thing going on."

"Flo Rida?" His mouth gaped open as he stared at her. "Are you fucking serious? You're comparing me to a rapper?"

Sawyer stepped over, leaning a hip on Mallory's desk. "You can be Doc Holiday if it makes you feel better."

Cole glared at him. "Now you're just being cruel."

Mallory smiled over at him. "How about we call you Agent C, like in *Men in Black*."

Cole shook his head as he headed for the coffee room. "I just know I'm going to regret this. You'd best be careful or I'll be the one murdering both your asses."

Mallory laughed. "Ah, but you say it so nicely, Cole."

Sawyer grinned at her as Cole disappeared into the room, still muttering to himself, and leaned in close. "Did you mean what you said in there? About 'til death?"

"Afraid so, baby. Looks like you're stuck with me."

"I'll find a way to cope. Just promise me one thing?"

"What's that?"

"You won't really let Cole sleep in the middle."

"Deal."

About the Author

Author, single mother, slave to chaos—she's a jack-of-all-trades who's constantly looking for her ever elusive clone.

Kris started writing some years back, and it took her a while to realise she wasn't destined for the padded room, and that the voices chattering away in her head were really other characters trying to take shape—and since they weren't telling her to conquer the human race, she went with it. Though she supposes if they had…insert evil laugh.

Kris loves writing erotic novels. She loves heroines who kick butt, heroes who are larger than life and sizzling sex scenes that leave you feeling just a bit breathless.

Kris Norris loves to hear from readers. You can find her contact information, website details and author profile page at http://www.totallybound.com.

Totally Bound Publishing

www.ingramcontent.com/pod-product-compliance
Lightning Source LLC
Chambersburg PA
CBHW030140180626
46812CB00002B/771